Abigail's Story

WOMEN OF THE BIBLE

Abigail's Story

ANN BURTON

A SIGNET BOOK

SIGNET
Published by New American Library, a division of
Penguin Group (USA) Inc., 375 Hudson Street,
New York, New York 10014, USA
Penguin Group (Canada), 10 Alcorn Avenue, Toronto,
Ontario M4V 3B2, Canada (a division of Pearson Penguin Canada Inc.)
Penguin Books Ltd., 80 Strand, London WC2R 0RL, England
Penguin Ireland, 25 St. Stephen's Green, Dublin 2,
Ireland (a division of Penguin Books Ltd.)
Penguin Group (Australia), 250 Camberwell Road, Camberwell, Victoria 3124,
Australia (a division of Pearson Australia Group Pty. Ltd.)
Penguin Books India Pvt. Ltd., 11 Community Centre, Panchsheel Park,
New Delhi - 110 017, India
Penguin Group (NZ), cnr Airborne and Rosedale Roads, Albany,
Auckland 1310, New Zealand (a division of Pearson New Zealand Ltd.)
Penguin Books (South Africa) (Pty.) Ltd., 24 Sturdee Avenue,
Rosebank, Johannesburg 2196, South Africa

Penguin Books Ltd., Registered Offices:
80 Strand, London WC2R 0RL, England

First published by Signet, an imprint of New American Library,
a division of Penguin Group (USA) Inc.

ISBN 0-7394-5108-1

For Mary Balogh

CHAPTER

1

Ｍy father, Oren, taught me that we begin as the clay dropped on the wheel of life. That the Adonai, the Lord-Who-Protects our people, brings us thus forth so that we might know His will. Throughout the turning of our lives, we are shaped beneath faith's exacting hands, adorned by the thin slip of our dreams, and seasoned in the kiln of our years.

After forty years of creating pots from far humbler clay, my father had a special understanding of our purpose and pondered it often. "If we are strong, my daughter," he would say, "then we are made useful."

I, too, worshipped the Adonai, but I thought more about how to sell our pottery at market. Being strong and useful was easier when we had a roof over our heads and enough food to eat.

"Greetings, Abigail," Shomer the rug seller called out to me as I made my way to my family's booth on the east end of the market. Carmel was not a large town, but because it lay between the wilderness of

Judah and the Negev Desert, many traveled through our region and stopped to trade at our gates; thanks to this, our market thrived.

"Greetings, Master Shomer." Before I reached the rug maker's stall, an old man moved into my path. He was one of the gerum, people who had no kin. Because gerum also had no nahalah, the land belonging to family, they pitched tents on common land or dwelled in the caves in the hills.

I recognized the old man. He came into town often and took whatever work he could get, but when there was none, he had to beg for his bread.

As he did now. "Pardon, Mistress." He held out a thin, trembling hand. "Have you food to spare?"

I had not yet eaten myself, but he looked very hungry. As I could only name one brother and my parents as kin—the rest of our family had died before my birth—I felt a special sympathy toward those who had none.

"I do." I placed half of the bread and goat cheese I had brought with me into his hands. "Peace be upon you, Rea."

My respectful tone and calling him my neighbor made him stand a little taller. "Bless you, Mistress." He hobbled off, following a well-trodden path to his solitary place by the beggar's gate.

Sorrow tightened my throat, for hunger, poverty, and loneliness were things my people understood only too well. I did not understand why, even when my father insisted that the centuries of suffering made us worthy of the One and True God. It was

what tempered and fired us. Those found unworthy
were discarded, their souls as useless as shattered
jugs.

If that was so, then I was sure that the Adonai had
a mountain of Hebrew potsherd somewhere.

My people had always worshipped the One and
True God, as far back as the time of legends, when
Hebrews had been made to build the great funerary
tombs for the Pharaohs of Egypt. The Adonai had
freed us of that yoke of slavery, and through Moses
had brought us into Canaan, where we spread out
over the land and grew like endless fields of wheat.
Our people were given the Promised Land, my father
said, because we had earned it. Whatever we wanted,
the Adonai would provide for us here.

My parents must not have wanted much, for the
Adonai had given us little more than the gerum.

When I stopped at Shomer's stall, the rug seller
immediately scolded me for my generosity. "You
should not be feeding your breakfast to beggars."

"I had enough for two," I said.

I liked Shomer, who was stout and good-natured,
the father of many sturdy sons and daughters. He
also spoke for all the lesser merchants before the
town's leaders at the monthly qahal, and the assembly gave his words respectful weight. He was kind,
as well. His stall was one of the busiest at market,
yet Shomer always spared a moment to greet me and
inquire after my family.

"Still, others could better afford to feed the poor,
Abigail." Shomer gave the wealthy oil merchant at

the other end of the market a disgusted look. He had
still not forgiven the other man for cheating his buyers by adding cheaper flaxseed oil to his casks.

"But they might not bring something for you." I
handed him a small sack.

"What have we here?" The rug seller peeked inside and uttered a startled laugh. "Madder root." He
took out one fat, twisted piece and held it up to
admire. "Queen of Heaven, where in Judah did you
find it?"

"Near the sycamore with the split trunk at the
mouth of the east spring," I told him. I had discovered it the night before, when I had taken our goats
out to graze on the sweet green grass that grew there.
"I saw plenty more to be had."

Madder root produced a rich, red dye that was far
easier and less costly to make than tola'at shani, the
dye extracted from a scarlet worm. Red was a popu-
lar color, too, for the rug seller was always seeking
out new sources to replenish his dye vats.

"For this I shall ask my wife to weave you a fine
new mantle," Shomer declared.

"There is no need." My old mantle was serviceable
enough, and the madder had cost me nothing but a
few moments of digging and dirty hands. "If she has
a blanket to spare, though, my mother would be glad
of it." The nights had been growing cold of late, and
Chemda's old blanket had worn thin in the center.

"I shall send the softest we have made over to
your father's house this morning," Shomer assured
me. "You are sure that is all you need?"

"Yes." What I truly needed he could not give. "My thanks, Master Shomer."

I felt ashamed that I even had to ask for the blanket in return, but my mother did need it, and I could not afford to buy one.

The poor circumstances in which my family lived had not seemed so terrible when I was a child. Small girls pay no heed to things such as the cost of food and shelter, not when there are wildflowers to pick and butterflies to chase. My parents also made what little we had seem like everything, and until I was older, I did not see how much they sacrificed to give Rivai and me nourishing meals and a decent home.

If only we could remain children forever, happy and unaware.

Over the years, deprivation and hard work shaped my parents, working on them in different ways. By the time I grew into womanhood, my mother and father had the silver hair and stooped walk of old ones. My carefree days of chasing butterflies had ended much earlier, when my mother's mind began to wander, and my father's fingers grew swollen and twisted.

When Oren grew too crippled to walk without a crutch, our neighbor, Cetura, brought me for the first time to the market outside the walls of our town to sell our pottery.

"Abigail need not go," Father had insisted, even after exhaustion from his last trip to market forced him to remain on his sleeping mat for two days. Like all Hebrew men, he thought it improper for an un-

married woman to sell at market. "I shall heal, and the Adonai will provide."

"You are not injured, and the Adonai does not have to eat or pay taxes," Cetura pointed out in her usual blunt fashion. "You do. Look upon yourself, Oren. You know the swelling in your joints will never go away. It is always so."

As first born, Rivai should have taken over for Father. My brother was a dreamer, however, and had already shown himself to be hopeless at potting and trading. All he was really good at was whittling bits of wood and bone, and watching over our mother, who could no longer be trusted to be left alone.

"Let Abigail come with me," our neighbor urged. "I shall teach her and watch over her, as if she were my own daughter. All will be well, I promise you."

My father had reluctantly given his consent.

Those first weeks I had been terrified of making a mistake, but Cetura had kept her word and watched over me, and I learned the business of buying and selling.

That had been two years ago.

Now I moved with confidence as I followed the center market aisle to the end, greeting other merchants on the way to where my father's booth stood. Unlike Shomer, who hung his wife's and daughters' beautifully woven rugs and blankets from a large, permanent stall built to his specifications, my family could afford only to rent one of the flimsy trade booths at the market's end.

Such booths as ours were fashioned cheaply: rough boards laid across stacks of broken, discarded brick

to form a three-sided, temporary square nestled against the town's stone wall. There was no roof to it, but the shadow of the wall kept all but the midday sun off my head, and market ended each day at that noon hour when the heat and light were strongest.

All I did to display our wares was to place the strings of pots on top of the boards. When someone wished to buy, I unknotted the slip-looped knot binding the desired pot to the cord. At the end of the day, I gathered what barter I had taken in trade, wrapped it in my shawl, hung the cords of unsold pots over my shoulders, and carried it all home.

I had another reason for liking the booth, as it was built next to the stall of Amri, a spice merchant. His herbs and spices lent to the air an exotic, ever-changing fragrance, which I enjoyed. There were leaves of dark green mint, crumbled stalks of dill, pungent white and black cumin seed, lacey rue with its tiny dried yellow flowers, and the sharp, flavorful scent of mustard leaves. Salt, brought by caravan from the sea, glittered from small boxes like stars.

Often Amri's customers would linger to enjoy the intriguing scents, too, and while there, some took notice of my pots and bought from me.

This morning I found my market neighbor hanging braids of garlic bulbs from tall, pegged stakes driven into the soil at the front corners of his stall. Short and thin, with a somewhat scraggly beard, Amri scowled as he went about his work.

This was not unusual. Nearly everything but buyers made the spice merchant glower.

"Good morning to you, Amri."

"What is so good about it?" He immediately glared down his smudge of a nose at me. "Olive prices are rising, as are taxes. Rainwater has seeped into my walls, and they must be repaired. For what the mason charges? I could *build* a new house."

Poor Amri. He particularly hated anything that came between him and his profits.

"I am sorry." I gave him a sympathetic smile. "I did bring those pots that you wanted." I lifted the cord that held the ten juglets with wooden plugs my brother had carved to fit the narrow necks. "Ten, as you said, with cedar stoppers." Unbaked clay balls sealed better, but the spice merchant preferred small, fancy touches that might better catch the eye of a wandering shopper. My brother had enjoyed carving the bits of cedar much more than turning the wheel for the jugs.

If only there were a market for carvings. One of the Adonai's ten sacred commandments forbade the making of pesel, however, and as a result Hebrews avoided anything with graven images. Rivai never liked selling his carvings anyway, so it mattered little.

"More for me to carry home," he grumbled. "What do you want for them?"

We merchants always bartered with each other; as with our customers it made more sense for us to trade goods instead of silver. At home we needed garlic for cooking, and soon I would use the last of the kushtha to make the unguent that eased the pain

of my father's aching joints. It was sensible to trade
for that.

Yet just this morning my mother had yearned
aloud for spice curls, doughy sweet rolls with a filling of honey, nuts, and ground sweet bark. They
were a luxury that I had not been able to make for
her for some time.

I knew the ingredients to make the rolls were
costly, and plain barley bread cheaper and more
nourishing, but my mother asked for so little, and
she never complained when she did without.

If I could stretch out the kushtha with warm oil
and fig poultices for my father's hands . . . "Have
you any sweet bark?"

"Some, but not much." Amri wanted the best of
any trade, so he constantly made as if running low
on everything. "Five quills for the pots."

"I would be beaten if I accepted so little." Actually
my father knew nothing about this order. My brother
and I had made the juglets, working late after my
parents had gone to sleep, but this I could not tell
the merchant. Men were potters, not women, and if
Amri knew the work to be mine, he would think the
juglets inferior. "Ten quills and a braid of garlic."

"You would see me starve away to a stick." He
released a heavy sigh. "Six quills, half a braid, and
your father makes a new water jug for me."

Bartering was an art of words, timing, and attitude.
I said nothing but frowned at my fingernails. The
frown was genuine; my hands looked deplorable,
roughened by secret hours at the wheel, faint traces

of red, dried clay under my nails. No matter how hard I scrubbed, the stain of my illicit work never went away.

I fought back the guilt that clung just as tenaciously. *It is not sinful. It is necessary.*

My father's hands, crippled as they were now, could only fashion the simplest vessels, such as flat eating bowls and saucers for lipped oil lamps. I would have to make the jug myself, which meant cajoling Rivai again to turn the wheel. This he hated, because it roughened *his* sensitive hands.

Thinking of my brother strengthened my resolve to make a decent trade. "Seven, a full braid, and I shall ask Father to work two handles on the jug."

Amri frowned. Cautious as he was, he knew a good trade when he saw one. "The jug would have to be seasoned, and filled."

Each morning I went to draw water from the community well for my parents and brother. Filling one more jar would be no great privation. Convincing Rivai to share the work of making the small pots had been much harder.

"For seven quills and a whole braid I shall deliver it full." I could see him still wavering, so I squelched a sigh and added, "And keep it filled for a week hence."

Amri was a bachelor and hated going to the well, where all the women gathered to gossip. He had no slaves—too expensive to keep, or so he claimed—so he was forced to take care of himself. Men did not

usually do such work, and the women always teased him about it.

A week of having his water delivered daily proved, as I'd suspected, a temptation he could not resist. "Done."

We clasped hands in merchant fashion to seal the trade.

"My thanks." I slipped the cord holding his juglets from my shoulder and held it out to him.

"How pretty." Cetura admired my handiwork as she shuffled past us with her barrow filled with brown-and-white barley. Although I was an experienced merchant now, she still checked on me every morning. "Come to see me at end of day, Abi. I need a new bread bowl before Shabbat, and I would have your father make it the same as the old."

I nodded. Cetura must have suspected that I now also made most of the pots I sold, although I did not fear she would expose me. She had been widowed young and had worked all her life to provide for her two sons, now grown. She had taught me that women at the market especially watched out for each other.

"Witch!"

"I will kill you, old hag!"

"Stop her!"

CHAPTER

2

Amri, Cetura, and I all turned around toward the angry shouts from the merchant's gate. It was not unusual to hear voices raised when the townspeople came to haggle, but it was early yet, barely a glimmer past dawn. Our customers were still abed or seeing to breaking their fast.

The lack of light made it difficult to spot the bent-over old woman at first, until she dodged the fruit seller's cart and changed direction to run our way. Dressed in rags she was, stick-thin and bareheaded as a poor beggar, but she moved with a thief's agility and cunning, head turning with quick jerks as if she were searching for better avenues, limbs tucked in to prevent collisions.

Behind her came three of the town's shamar on foot, their swords drawn and flashing in the brimming sunlight. Like all the men who guarded Carmel, they were large, muscular, and not concerned

about what they broke in pursuit of justice, whether stall fronts, melons, or heads.

Amri jumped over the side slat of his stall and huddled over as many jars, skins, and packets as he could to protect his investment. "Adonai yireh."

Our Lord might protect the spice merchant's soul, but from the way the shamar were crashing through the market, all of our wares were definitely at risk.

"Cetura," I said as I watched one guardsman knock over the fruit merchant's cart, creating a slippery flood of ripened dates, "move your barrow over there before it is tipped." I nodded toward the space behind a booth two places from mine.

My neighbor followed my advice, and so I stood alone when the old fugitive tried to run around me. When confronted by the sight of the green and white hills beyond the town, the thief came to a dead stop and staggered back as if aghast. Her right side collided with my strings and made two pots fall. I caught one in time, but the other hit the sun-baked ground and smashed into pieces.

The sound seemed to make everyone around us freeze, for it was very bad luck to smash a new pot. Some believed that if you inscribed the name of an enemy on an unused pot and then deliberately broke it, it was as a curse upon the one named.

I did not believe in such things, but I did not rejoice in the loss of my wares. We were not rich, my family and I, and selling pottery kept bread on our table and the roof over our heads. This old one obviously could not pay for her carelessness.

"Be still," I scolded her. My warning was not an idle one, for she was as barefoot as I, and sharp potsherds glittered on the ground for a yard around us. "Your feet shall be torn to ribbons if you try to flee now."

"They mean to kill me." Her voice held no terror, only the rasp of exhaustion.

"We do not put criminals to death here." But the shamar were within their rights to cut off her right hand, and the shock and indignity of that often did away with the older ones. I peered into her face, but her unkempt, filthy white hair masked it. I had no love of thieves, but something about her made me ask, "What have you done?"

"Offered truth where only lies were welcome." Burning eyes, like those of a mad dog, glittered from beneath the veil of hair. A gnarled hand seized my wrist, bruising it as she jerked me close. The smell of her was as fevered and unpleasant as her gaze. "You work the clay."

"No, I but sell the *pots*." I took a step back, but she kept hold of my arm. "Please release me." Why was I being so polite to a thief? My father, were he well enough to come to market these days, would have beaten her away with his crutch.

"The hand that works the clay shapes the world," she whispered, and flipped my wrist so that my palm faced up. She stared at it, jerked once, and peered into my eyes with something like outrage. "Wife you shall soon be. But whose?"

How could the thief have guessed I was unmar-

ried? My khiton, which was one of my mother's and plainly colored, marked me as a married woman. Since I had begun selling at market, I never wore a striped samla, the robe of a betulah, a young Hebrew maiden. The other merchants understood my home situation, and had never rebuked me for my small pretense.

Besides my garb, I was almost too old to be considered betulah anymore. In my heart I had accepted that no one would ever offer for me, for I would bring nothing to a marriage, no portion of animals or nahalah land. Bahur, the young Hebrew men eligible for marriage, expected something in return for the mohar, the normal price they paid to the family of their bride.

"You do not believe me."

I stared at the old thief. Perhaps she was as crazed as she was odorous. "I am not to marry."

"Yet." The broken edges of her crusted fingernails stabbed into my flesh. "For my debt to you, this is what I see: One king fool, one fool king." She appeared ready to collapse, but she would not release me. "Whose shall you be, and whose truth shall you speak?"

"I don't understand." My wrist hurt, though, and there would be bruises to explain if she did not turn me loose.

"You shall, Father's Delight. When you doubt, go back to the wheel. Turn the wheel." All the strength seemed to go out of her, and she sagged against me and groaned. "Turn the—"

"Hold!"

One of the shamar pulled me away while the other two seized the old woman. She fought them like one possessed of demons, scratching and writhing between them. "Misbegotten sons of Amel's countless whores! I conjured truth for him! I curse your souls to be devoured! May the snapping jaws of—"

A heavy leather gauntlet came down on her head, stunning her into silence and making blood spill over her lip.

"Please!" I reached out a hand to ward off a second blow. "She is too old; you shall kill her."

"Do not your eyes work, woman?" The guardsman who had struck the thief grabbed a fistful of her hair and jerked her head back, revealing her face for the first time. Foreign-looking dark blue tattoos of spirals circled her cheeks and brow, but her skin had the unlined, early bloom of youth.

Whoever she was, from wherever she had come, she was not Hebrew. Uneasy now, I drew back a step. "Who is she?"

"A m'khashepah," the guard said, and released the thief's hair. Her head drooped against her chest. "She stole a jeweled chalice from Shofet Choab and fled his house."

Choab was a powerful man, a town leader and a judge who had the ear of King Saul himself. A descendent of the tribe of Aaron, he held sway over many of the shofetim in our region for twenty years, making him a judge of judges. He also served the king as a military commander in times of war. Some

said the shofet broke Hebrew law as often as he adjudicated it, but he was not a man with whom one trifled, or of whom one made an enemy.

Stealing from the shofet was a terribly grievous offense; for that—and practicing witchcraft within the walls of the town—the thief would likely be sold into slavery.

Yet something was wrong with this charge. I looked her over. Her ragged garments possessed no hidden pockets or folds where something so large and expensive could be concealed. "She carries no chalice."

"Likely she hid it somewhere ere she fled, intending to retrieve it later. It matters not. Her lies will earn her chains." The largest shamar hefted the thief under his arm like a limp sack of grain.

"Wait." I felt oddly indebted to the thief/m'khashepah, but what could I do? To gain an audience with Choab took weeks, and then only a man could petition the minister. My father was not well enough to do so, and Rivai wouldn't care about an issah nokriyah, a foreign female, especially not one accused of thievery and witchcraft.

Feeling helpless and foolish, I crouched down and laid my hand on the lolling, white head. *What had been done to her, to steal the color from her hair and the sanity from her mind?* "I am sorry, but I cannot help you in this. I shall pray to the Adonai to have mercy on you."

Her head lifted sluggishly. "You are a generous and merciful one." Those burning eyes dimmed a

little as they met mine, but she focused, and then she bared strong white teeth in a ferocious, slightly mad smile. "Yes, mercy, that is it. Seek mercy where none is deserved. Cry mercy when none is earned. Stand and you shall fall. Kneel and you shall rise. Search for it, bargain for it, crawl for it. . . ." The last word ended in a furious shriek as she began fighting the guardsman again.

My hands trembled as I watched the shamar drag her from the marketplace. My palm felt wet, and I looked down to see bright red blood on my palm. I stared at it, horrified even more when I realized it must have come from the other woman's head.

We do not put criminals to death here, I had assured her. Would Shofet Choab make a liar of me?

"Here." Amri's shaking hand thrust a bit of rag cloth into mine. He was making protective signs over himself with the other hand and staring in the direction the guardsmen had dragged the m'khashepah.

"Go and wash, Abigail," Cetura urged me in a tight, horrified voice. "Scrub every trace of that evil one from your hands."

The blood washed away easily enough, but the memory of it would not. Nor would the m'khashepah's words leave my thoughts, though I could make no sense of them.

Stand and you shall fall. Kneel and you shall rise.

The early uproar at the market created a demand for pots, for many more than my own had been smashed. I took some trade in return, but from those

merchants whose wares had been ruined, I accepted a promise of payment.

"But I do not know when I can pay," Geddel the clothes mender said after he asked for my largest scrub basin to replace the one the shamar had smashed. The mended garments at his stall had been trampled in the dirt, and all of them needed washing before they were returned to their owners.

I knew Geddel had an extended family to feed, and his kin lived far to the north. He worked very long hours, both at home and at the market, and I suspected that he and his lived, as my family did, from hand to mouth.

"I meant to visit your wife and see the new baby," I told him impulsively. "Let this be my birth-gift for him."

Geddel lifted his eyebrows. "Our *new* baby walks on his own now, Abigail."

I gave his shoulder a friendly pat. "Then you must tell your wife that I am sorry the gift is late."

When all the pots I had brought but one were gone, I left the market, stopping at the communal well to use my last pot to draw water before continuing home.

"No strings of leftovers today, Abigail?" Ketina, the youngest daughter of Huram the coppersmith, asked as she took her turn at the well to fill her water jars.

Like other young girls, Ketina came to draw water several times daily. She had a lively disposition that suited her merry little face. The latter had been sun-

spattered with freckles from going outside without a head cloth, much to the despair of her mother.

"I sold everything, praise the Adonai." The words sounded lifeless even to my own ears, and I forced a smile. "How does your family fare?"

"All is shouting and wailing this day." The girl's big brown eyes rolled before she leaned close and lowered her voice. "My brother Tzalmon wishes to pledge his troth to Devash, the shepherd Noisan's girl, but her father doesn't approve of the match."

Tzalmon was a handsome young man and a good friend of my brother's. He could be somewhat brash while in Rivai's company, but Huram's influence showed in Tzalmon's genial manners, and his mother's influence in the respect he always showed older women.

I thought Devash could do much worse than Ketina's brother. "Why does Devash's father disapprove?"

"We're not sure—no one will say outright—but I think it is the mohar her father asks," Ketina said, her voice lowering to a murmur. "Tzal is still apprenticed to Gowen the stonecutter, you know, and although he no longer has to pay his master's fees he must earn his room and board, so little is left over. There are fifteen of us at home, so Father can help only so much. Noisan lives modestly, and Devash is his only daughter. It is said that she shall bring land and many sheep to her husband."

I had not known Devash so endowered. That meant the bride price she commanded would proba-

bly be more than the usual fifty silver sheqels. "I am sorry to hear it."

"Tzal should know better, but these days his heart rules his head." The girl lifted her shoulders. "Mother is beside herself, but when is she not? Father says it is the Lord's will and then goes into the smith to hammer on something."

My father also went to the wheel whenever Rivai railed over our lack of wealth. "Perhaps he may save until he can afford her." As an apprentice Tzalmon could improve his situation in time, but for my brother, who refused to learn an acceptable trade, choices would always be limited.

"By then she shall be too old and worn . . ." She trailed off, suddenly embarrassed.

To give him sons, was what she meant to say. Too old and worn out, as I would soon be.

I had never been courted, not even once, for my father had no zebed of nahalah land or herd animals to offer. Such a dowry was vital, for eligible young bahur expect a wife to add her portion to the family holdings.

If the Adonai had fashioned me with bold colors or a fetching shape, then I might have caught the eye of a young man. Sometimes I dreamed of myself in a different body, one of great beauty and grace, surrounded by countless handsome young bahur, treasured and admired by all.

When I woke, I was still plain, sturdy Abigail of Carmel, as useful and ordinary as a table jug.

"No matter," I said, keeping my tone even. "One as handsome as your brother shall find another easily."

"As you say." Gladly she changed the subject. "You should take a rest when you get home, Abi, you look very tired."

And old. And worn out.

"I am well." Well or not, I would take no rest for some hours yet. Waiting for me at home was grain to grind and the garden to tend and the goats to graze and water and the evening meal to make. And if I felt as if a hundred pickling jars hung from my shoulders, what of it? There was no one else to carry my unseen burdens. Unlike Tzalmon, I had no betrothed over whom to agonize, and I was beginning to think that I never would.

Wife you shall soon be . . . but whose?

The prediction made me feel sick, sick of myself and my secret yearnings. I was fortunate that I had a little house with a patch of garden, and two goats, and a loving family. It may not have been much, but it was more than the m'khashepah would have, once Choab sold her to slavers to recover his losses. Imagining her life from there made me shudder.

"Here." Ketina brought up the heavy bucket and before I could protest, filled my water jar for me. "That's one less task for you to do."

I touched her arm with gratitude, but her kindness made me feel sad. *If only I had a sibling like her.* "My thanks, little friend."

CHAPTER
3

After I bid Ketina good-bye, I adjusted my strings and braced the heavy water jug on my hip, then made my way from the well to my home. Carmel was a clean and pleasant town, but it was not a very exciting place. It was neither the richest nor poorest town in Judah, with merely dirt roads and modest mud-brick dwellings, the inhabitants more industrious than friendly. They had to be; most homes contained three or four generations under one roof, along with the family's goats, sheep, and workrooms.

My brother thought our town not very grand at all.

"We should move to a city in the north, where the avenues are paved with stone and beasts do the hauling," Rivai had told my father more than once. "They say there are fountains and two-story houses with floors of river pebble and courtyards with gardens of flowers where artists can dream. Musicians play day and night but for the joy of it!"

My father usually nodded absently, hearing but

not hearing Rivai, but during one such tirade he had given him a weary look. "We cannot dine on dreams or joy, my son. We must earn our keep."

"The soul needs more than barley gruel and water!" my brother snapped back before storming up the ladder to the roof.

Rivai spent much time on the roof. Sometimes I wondered if he went up there to brood, or to place himself above us. Perhaps our roof was the closest thing to the balcony of the grand house in which my brother felt he deserved to dwell, where his soul could feast on the joy of creating something for nothing.

He would be good at that, I thought, allowing myself a moment of rare bitterness. *If only idle pleasures were a trade.*

Today I was home early and found my father dozing outside in his hammock. Our home was square and only a single level, with four small rooms and an open-sided niche shaded by a canopy of boughs and brushwood. Through the niche I walked to the center of the house, which needed a new roof and was really too small to be called a proper courtyard. There I checked the round clay oven to make sure the coals from breakfast were still hot, and added some twigs from a large pile of brushwood I collected on my walks and kept neatly stacked in one corner.

I carried the water jug into our front room, the largest space in the house, where we ate and worked and where I slept. As firstborn and son, Rivai was

entitled to his own room, and my parents shared the other. The fourth room opened out to the niche, so we used it to store the heavy pallets of red and gray potting clay, and to bed down the goats at night.

Automatically I washed my bare feet before stepping onto the beaten-clay floor.

"Mother?" I removed my outer mantle and head cloth and walked back to my parents' chamber, but found it empty. I heard soft singing and followed it to the storage room. There my mother sat on the straw-covered floor, between our two goats, an arm around the spotted hide of the smaller, rocking a little as she murmured an old cradle tune. The second goat lay asleep at her side, and I saw that she had draped her head cloth over it as one might over a slumbering infant.

This bizarre sight was not at all a surprise to me. I had seen many like it over the last few years.

Chemda, my mother, was said to have once been a very handsome woman, but hard work and several miscarriages had left her frail and thin. She was not feebleminded, exactly, but she had not been right, not since the last time she had lost a baby. Her thoughts often wandered in odd directions, and things she said and did sometimes made little sense. She also suffered from frightening spells of forgetfulness; on some bad days she did not know me, my brother, my father, or even her own name.

I prayed today was not one of those days. "Mother," I called to her again. I kept my voice gentle and remained where I was, in the doorway. When

she had her spells, often loud voices or sudden movements terrified her.

Chemda looked up, her clouded eyes nearly crossing until she focused on my face. "Abigail." She glanced at a shaft of sun streaming in through the room's small window. "You are home early."

"Yes, Mother." Relief made me smile as I came forward to help her up from the floor. "All our pots sold quickly today." I reached for her head cloth.

"How nice. Oren shall be pleased. Don't do that." She gave my hand a slap. "You might wake the babe."

I left the head cloth where it was and did not argue with her. Over time she had told me that both of the goats, the birds that nested in the courtyard, and even some large stones were my siblings. It was easy enough to indulge her whimsies until she forgot about this day's pretend babies.

I guided my mother out to the front room and gave her a rusk spread with date honey to snack on while I swept the floor and worked on preparing the evening meal. I set a pot of broth with lentils, onions, and garlic to heat on the cooking fire, and then mixed and shaped barley flour dough to make two large lehem, the wheel-shaped rounds of bread we ate on ordinary days. I saved what little fine wheat flour and honey we could afford to make a special sweet loaf for Shabbat dinner.

"It is good of you to make the meal," my mother said, as formally as if I were a guest. "May I help?"

"Of course." I gave her a bowl of figs I had taken

in trade at market. Picking them over was busy work, but if she cooked, inevitably her attention wandered off with her thoughts, and things burned. Shadows stretched across the room as the sun dropped behind the hills.

"Where is Rivai?" Even if my brother had gone over to Shomer's house to commiserate with Tzalmon, he should have been home by now.

"These figs are too green, child. You shall give yourself a sour belly if you eat them." She peered at my loaves, saw that I had pinched off a bit of dough to save in the leavening jar for tomorrow's baking, and nodded her approval. "Who is this Rivai?"

"Our son, Chemda." My father, Oren, hobbled in, leaning heavily on his crutch.

Once my father had seemed like the strongest man in the world to me: tall, broad of shoulder, with long, tireless arms and clever, callused hands. Though he worked at the wheel every day, he held his back straight and his head high and proud. His were the eyes of a dreamer, deep brown and gentle, oh, so gentle. As a child I would tug at his thick, curly brown beard with my little hands whenever he carried me, until he would use it to tickle my neck and make me giggle.

Those memories made it all the harder to look upon my father as he was now. Age, work, and worry had caused him to shrink in on himself like a poorly thrown jug, his shoulders slumping, his back permanently curved, his head sunken on his neck. His once clever hands hung knotted and gnarled, the

fingers twisted, the joints as fat as overripe grapes. White streaked his hair and beard, and his dreamer's eyes were almost lost now in drooping, wrinkled folds.

"Dinner is almost ready, Father." On my way to the oven stones I gave him a kiss of welcome and felt the tension in his shoulders. *The pain must be very bad today.* After I left the loaves to bake on the flat stones in the center of the oven, I asked him, "Would you like a cup of tea?" I had enough kushtha left to brew a strong remedy, which I would flavor with coriander to mask the taste of the medicinal herb, and by which he would pretend to be fooled.

Dignity was vital to my father, and preserving his was everything to me.

"My thanks, Daughter." He came to sit on the bench by our table and saw the empty strings. "Trade was brisk today?"

For a moment, I debated on whether to tell him about my strange encounter with the m'khashepah, but he already worried over me going to market alone. "Very much so, Father. I sold all but one."

Rather than reassure him, that seemed to make the worry lines bracketing his mouth deeper. "I shall have to spend some extra hours at the wheel this night."

That he could not do, not without crippling himself for the next week.

"We also have some special orders from two of the merchants," I told him, "who asked for Rivai's

work. I promised he would fill them as soon as possible."

My father gave me a sharp look. "Your brother is out with those Egyptian friends of his."

That meant Rivai would be drinking and gambling, two more things he did with little restraint or skill.

"He and I shall work later." To hide my dismay, I stirred the soup. "It is cooler and quieter then, anyway."

When our father first began to suffer from joint pain, I made a bargain with my brother. Rivai would turn the big stone wheel for me, but I would let everyone think that the pots I made were his handiwork. He had agreed—reluctantly—and only because I offered him part of what I took in trade. Profit always outweighed Rivai's sense of masculine outrage.

Lately, it had outweighed everything.

I brought in the baked lehem from the outdoor oven, set our meal on the table, and joined hands with my parents as my father said the blessing. Worry over my brother and the words of the m'khashepah slipped away as I gave thanks for the food.

What we had might be humble, but it was ours, and it was enough.

My parents went to sleep early that night, but I stayed up to tidy the house, milk the goats, and wait for Rivai. He had not arrived home by the time I finished inside the house, so I sat in the garden and watched the stars appear in the night sky.

I always watched them alone.

My parents were not of a noble line, and famine and sickness had taken all their kin. What little surplus we had was saved for Rivai, so that someday he might offer something for his future bride, if he ever found one.

This I knew, and accepted, but to my great shame, I still prayed for a husband.

It was a habit of which no one knew. Every night I sat among the herbs and vines and begged Adonai to bless me with an offer. I did not even ask for a young and handsome man anymore. I knew myself; I would be satisfied with a simple man of modest means, a companion and protector who would give me a home to care for and babies to love. A lesser merchant, a shamar, even a farm worker or shepherd would have satisfied me.

I could not depend on Rivai to look after me, not when he had no trade or wife. I did not want to die alone, an old and unloved woman begging or dependent on the charity of others. I wanted a home of my own, and many children to love, and I could not have those without a husband.

Wife you will be.

This night I had no entreaty for the Adonai; the thief's foolish words had torn a veil from my eyes. It was time I accepted my lot. I had nothing, and I could not leave my parents to Rivai's uncertain care.

I would be alone forever.

A scuffling sound came from the street, and then I heard my brother singing. With haste I tucked my

head cloth around my face and hurried out to the front of the house. There, two strange men stood with my brother, who was staggering on his feet and bleeding from his nose.

"Two days," one of the men said before he shoved Rivai at me.

I caught Rivai by the arms and dug my heels in before his weight knocked us both over. My brother stood as tall as our father had in his youth, but thankfully was much leaner. His khiton was torn and spotted with blood, while his breath smelled of strong wine. When I looked over his shoulder, the two men had gone.

"Abigail." Rivai clutched at me as if unable to stand on his own. He gave me a silly grin. "My favorite sister."

"Your only sister." I grabbed him as he lurched. *Too much to drink again.* I helped him inside, eased the door shut, and kept my voice low so as not to wake our parents. "What happened? Were you in a fight?" Someone had obviously hit him in the face, for his nose and lower lip were red and swollen.

"My ribs," he gasped when I caught him again to keep him from falling over. "Are they broken?"

I gently touched his sides to check, but felt no ominous swelling or shifting of bone. "I think only bruised. Rivai, what did that man mean?"

"What man? Why does the room spin like a top?" My brother collapsed at the table, his breathing choppy as he gripped the edge. "Bring me wine and go to bed."

"You are sitting in my bedroom, and I think you have had enough to drink." I brought him water instead. "Who did this to you? Were you robbed?"

"That is it. Yes." He sipped from the cup. "I was robbed by Maon scum." Absently he wiped his nose with the back of his hand. The sight of the blood seemed to surprise him. "I should bathe." He tried to rise, but his face paled and he abruptly dropped down again. "Maybe later."

I saw fresh blood trickle from his nostrils and brought a damp cloth for him. "Is your nose broken?"

He used the cloth gingerly. "Almost. Cowards. They ganged up on me, you know. Four on one." He felt the middle part of his nose. "Or maybe it was five."

"I shall wake Father." We Carmelites generally avoided people from the nearby town of Maon, and they did the same with us. If they were coming here to rob our men, then Father would notify the shofet. Choab would take quick action and ban the wretches from entering our gates.

Before I could go to my parents' room, Rivai reached out and seized my wrist. "Do not wake him, Abi. I was not robbed." He grimaced. "Not exactly."

"What happened to you, then, exactly?"

He shrugged. "I went to Maon with Nefat, and we stopped at a gaming hall."

Maon was a settlement built on a high hill a mile to the south of our town. It was a rough place frequented by sheepherders and shearers from Ziph and

Juttah. Maon was where they spent their wages on drink, gaming, and the Adonai knew what else.

To my knowledge, my brother had never been there before. "Father does not permit you to go there."

"I am a man now, Abi. Father does not own me." He felt his nose again. "It *is* almost broken, those dogs. A debt is no reason to beat a man. I told them I would pay it."

"You have a debt?" My brother had never gambled outside our town or wagered more than he carried. We were too poor to merit credit from anyone. At least, I had thought we were.

"I was cheated." Rivai sat up and gave me an indignant glare. "The dice were switched, and the last were weighted, I swear it."

I still could not get past the fact that my brother had gambled beyond his means to pay and had been beaten for it. "How much do you owe?"

"A debt is a matter for men," he said, all haughty male now. "You would not understand."

Would I not? Who did he think managed the household income? Our mother? "Then I shall wake Father," I said, "and you two *men* can discuss it."

Again my brother moved to stop me. "No, please, Abi." His manly arrogance vanished, leaving behind only a frightened boy. "You cannot speak of this to him."

"I promise, I shall not." *Why is he so afraid?* I braced myself even as I reached out to take his hand in mine. "How much did you lose, Rivai?"

He looked at the table. "Eight."

"Eight pots or eight measures of emmer?" The pots we could begin making tonight and, if we worked late, have finished in two days. It would be harder to put together so much grain. I had earned two sacks of millet from today's trading; perhaps Cetura would exchange—

"Eight maneh of gold," Rivai said.

CHAPTER

4

Eight maneh of gold.
Rivai's words rang in my ears, and I felt as if my blood turned to clay. I barely felt his hand slip from my numb fingers.

"Gold." I could barely shape the word with my lips. "You gambled with *gold?*"

His head drooped before he nodded.

No, it could not be. We had no gold. We had never had any gold. There was a little silver, saved from the very best years, but no one was permitted to touch it. My father had put the silver aside to serve as mohar for my brother's future wife.

Gold was wholly beyond us.

"From where did you get this gold?" A more horrifying thought occurred to me. "You did not *steal* it?"

"I am no thief." Rivai gave me a highly offended look. "Nefat took me over to Maon to a gaming house. The man playing, Nabal, was drunk and making reck-

less plays. Nefat lent me enough to bet against him. I won the dice, and then the throw, and then I kept winning." He leaned over, lowering his voice to an excited whisper. "By moonrise he had lost twelve maneh of gold to me, enough to buy a house in the west quarter and you a husband. None of us would have had to work for the rest of our lives."

I stopped listening so that I could calculate. Twelve maneh were equal to six hundred gold sheqels, or a whole bar of gold, more wealth than I or anyone in our quarter could expect to see in a lifetime. It was a veritable fortune: a family of twenty could live in luxury on but half such an amount for as many years.

"You should have seen me play," my brother continued to boast. "Every throw was mine. Why, if I had—"

"You said you owe eight," I reminded him.

His shoulders slumped, and his face fell into a familiar, belligerent expression. "My luck turned, and that drunken fool began to win. I had to keep playing to recover what I had lost, didn't I?"

"So you lost your winnings plus eight you did not have to this Nabal." Who had likely not been drunk or a fool. "How could you do such a thing?"

"I was tricked," he insisted. "Nabal pressed me to drink. When my gold was gone, Nefat whined about the stake I owed him. I could not stop."

It was sounding more and more as if my brother had been swindled. "Is Nefat your friend, or Nabal's?"

"Nefat was taken in, the same as I." He scowled.

"I know why the Maon switched the dice. Nabal's losses made him fear my great luck."

"I am certain that it terrified him." I rested my throbbing forehead against my palm. "We have not eight silver sheqels to our name, Brother. How do you mean to repay this man?"

Rivai yawned. "I can borrow from friends."

"Friends like Tzalmon, who cannot afford to wed," I suggested, "or Klurdi, who has nearly beggared his parents with his own drinking and gaming?"

"Nefat will lend it to me." There was a new uncertainty in his eyes and voice. Perhaps my brother was only now realizing how few sensible friends he had. "Or someone else."

"Let us imagine no one can," I said. "What then? Will this Nabal have you arrested?" He shook his head and looked away from me. New dread poured atop the cold knot in my chest. "Rivai, what will he do to you if you cannot pay? *Tell* me."

"Maon law gives Nabal leave to take the debt owed from my family from our go'el," he muttered. "We have no kin to pay our debts, so it must come from Father."

We were not subject to Maon law unless we lived or worked in that town. However, Maon's distractions kept many undesirables away from Carmel, and I suspected that our shofetim would not bar the town's authorities from pursuing and prosecuting my brother, even from a suspected swindler.

"Our parents cannot pay this anymore than you can." No one in our quarter could.

My brother's mouth tightened. "Father could borrow from one of his friends."

"No one has the means to loan him that much, and we have nothing of value to serve as collateral. The house is practically worthless. The wheel, perhaps, might bring some money, and the goats; only then we would have no pots to sell or milk to . . ." The memory of mad, burning eyes silenced me. Under Hebrew law, those who could not pay their debts were considered equal to thieves. "Would Nabal force Father to sell one of us into slavery?"

My brother made a sound of contempt. "Don't talk foolishness, Abigail. For eight maneh, he would have to sell himself as well as you and me *and* Mother."

I knew the law. A man's debts had to be paid, however he obtained the payment. As long as we were healthy, we would go to the slave caravans.

"If you do not pay this debt, he shall be held responsible. He shall do what he must." Such a thing would break my father's failing spirit.

No, my heart informed me. *It shall kill him.* Long before the deprivations of life as a slave would.

"It is a *stupid* law," Rivai flared, slamming his fist into the table. He winced and shook it. "It matters not what the law says. I am a grown man. I shall give them what I can borrow, and Nabal will have to be satisfied with that until I can find the rest."

"And if he is not?"

My brother nursed his hand, his expression sulky. "I shall go to the shamar, then, and explain that it is not my fault, that the game was rigged—"

"When the shamar are finished laughing, they shall put us all in chains and lead us to the slave caravans." Too upset to remain still, I rose from the table. "Who is this Nabal?"

"He has the biggest herds of sheep and goats in Judah, and much property in Maon. They say no one has a tighter fist than Nabal, and that is why he has no wife or family or friends. Even his hired herdsmen are said to live like beggars." Rivai gave me a cautious look. "Are you going to tell Father?"

"I said I would not." I needed to think, and I could not do that by weeping and wailing over my brother's idiocy. "Come, wash and change out of your khiton. You must turn the wheel for me tonight."

My brother gaped. "You still mean to work?"

"There is no market for our tears," I said simply.

Eight maneh of gold.

As I walked to the storage room, the reality of the enormous debt seemed to loom over me like a towering ziggurat.

Which it was, compared to our extremely modest income. A very good week of selling at market earned us barter equal to perhaps two silver sheqels. Most of that I traded again to other merchants for what my family needed to live: food and medicines, dyes for cloth and clay, hardwood for the kiln, oil for the lamps, flax and wool for weaving, fodder for the goats . . .

Eight maneh. More gold than might be earned in *ten* good *years.*

The red clay used to make our pots was very smooth and pure, thanks to the clean water of the spring near the bank from which we took it. Once a month my brother and I borrowed one of our Shomer's carts to haul our pallets to the spring and refill them, a long and exhausting task that, like so many, had become too much for our father to perform.

What will we tell Father when the Maon's men come for payment?

Earlier in the week I had washed and tempered a large mound of red clay, treading it with my bare feet, which rendered it malleable enough for the wheel. From this I gathered as much as I could carry, and asked my brother to bring the jar of soft rainwater I used for slips and turnings.

My father's wheel occupied one corner of the courtyard, separated by screens woven of olive wood and goat hair rope. It was not a very large wheel, only six hands across, but it sat balanced perfectly on its stone axis and spun freely with the lightest of touches. Time and countless mounds of clay had worn the surface of the gray speckled stone disk to a satisfying smoothness.

Slaves, like women, were generally not permitted to make pots. In three days I might lose more than my personal freedom. I was no artisan like my brother, but working the clay pleased me. It made me feel that I was more than the one who cooked and cleaned and sold things.

Are these the last I shall ever make?

While I portioned out the clay, Rivai brought my

father's short stool and set it in place. He nudged the edge of the wheel, smearing some grease beneath to keep grit out of the axis seam, and took position behind it. Because turning the wheel meant he would be continually splattered by the clay and water it flung, he wore only an old ezor modestly wrapped around his hips.

"How long will this take?" he asked me. "I am weary."

He was weary. I had been awake and working since before dawn, and had done more than he would in a week. I felt so tired my bones ached, and now the thought of eight maneh of gold ground like olive press stones atop my fatigue.

For a moment I was tempted to throw the clay at my brother's head.

"As long as it takes." I put on one of my father's woolen work aprons to protect my khiton, dropped a portion of clay on the reed bat covering the top of the wheel, and dipped my hands in the rainwater.

Rivai sighed and bent to the wheel. Its edges were heavier than its center, so when it began to spin under his hands it continued revolving on its own for some time. In order for me to properly work the clay, all my brother had to do was give the moving wheel a push now and then to sustain an even rate of spinning.

Pain knotted beneath my breast. *If only a heart could be so effortlessly sustained.*

Fashioning pots was not as easy as it appeared. I had watched my father work at the wheel all my life,

and time and again he had allowed me to work my own little pots. Those were the happiest times I could remember, when he sat me on his stool, my short legs dangling, and spun the wheel for me. He had always treated me as if I were a master potter.

"You have clever hands, my daughter," he would say to me. "Ah, if only you were a boy."

For all my play on the wheel as a child, my first serious attempts had been laughably lopsided. It took many months of practice in secret before I was able to make something worth selling, and yet another season before I was skilled enough to create reasonable duplicates of my father's work.

From three mounds I worked utilitarian jars and lamps of sizes that I knew would sell well at market. These I made so often I could shape them with my eyes closed, leaving myself free to consider what to do about Rivai's impossible debt.

Rivai was right. We could not pay such a debt, not unless Father sold us and all we had. Even if our parents were spared lives as slaves, they would have to beg in the street for food until the shamar finally ran them out of the town. Unprotected in the wilderness, they would starve or be killed by wild animals, marauders, or the elements.

I would die before I allowed that to happen.

"We could flee to Hebron," my brother said, as if knowing my thoughts. "It is a city of refuge."

Rivai knew so little of the law. I, on the other hand, had learned much about it from other merchants as well as from those who passed through the market-

place. Knowledge I wished that I did not have, not on this night.

"Cities like Hebron are only for those who kill by accident, if they can persuade the gatekeepers that they are truly innocent," I told him. "Sanctuary is offered to protect a life, not a purse—or lack of one."

He gave the wheel a halfhearted push. "You despise me, don't you?"

I had often resented Rivai because my parents had indulged him so much, and because he had so much more freedom than I. I also secretly envied his carvings, which were much finer and more delicate than anything I could ever make. Even so, he was my brother.

"I do not always understand you, or the things you want," I admitted, "but I could never hate you."

"I wanted a good life, and the chance to make my art. Now I have probably ruined mine, and yours, and our parents'." He regarded me with suddenly sad eyes. "You should hate me. You deserve better than this endless work, with the three of us hanging on you, like ugly pots which you shall never sell."

My fingers clenched, inadvertently ruining the rim of the bowl I was shaping. "You and Mother and Father *are* my life," I said, trying not to sound defensive. "You have never been my burdens. What I do is done out of love for you."

"Love that you would rather give another. I've heard you in the courtyard at night, you know. You are too practical to believe the Adonai will actually

send you a husband, and you do nothing to find one yourself. Still, you yearn and pray." He shook his head. "I don't understand why you waste yourself on us, Abigail."

"Prayer, like hope, costs nothing." I had never considered looking for a husband; it was not something a woman did. Besides, without a zebed, who would have me? "You cannot say that about your gambling and drinking."

"You are right," Rivai said, startling me. "I am nothing but a wastrel, am I not? Yet whatever happens to me, I shall have some good memories to warm me through the cold, hard years ahead. What will you have?"

I would have my self-respect. Like prayer and hope, it was noble. Only now it did not feel very substantial. "It is late. We can stop." I took the lopsided bowl from the wheel and mixed it back into the remaining clay. "My thanks for your help."

His eyes glittered as he slowly straightened. With tears or anger, I could not say. "I shall think of a way out of this, Abi."

That was good, because I could not see one for the tears in my eyes.

After Rivai had gone to bed, I shelved the pots I had thrown so that they would dry overnight. In the morning I would put them, leathery hard, in the kiln for firing before I went to market. Since I could not tell my parents about Rivai's debt, I would ask advice of Shomer, or perhaps Amri or Cetura. They

were shrewd merchants as well as my friends. If anyone could help, they would.

As I shook out my bed mat, I ignored the voice
inside me that told me over and over that there was
no solution, no possible way to save Rivai or my
family.

Because the night was humid and hot, I put my
mat next to the wall beneath one of the windows. I
was always too tired to stay awake, even on the hot-
test nights, but now I tossed and turned, unable to
sink into the dark, blessed oblivion of sleep for several hours.

At last I slept and fell into a dream.

I found myself at our market booth. Beautiful pots
painted with all the colors of the rainbow sat in neat
rows, linked to each other by golden strings. They
were lovelier than anything I had ever fashioned, and
without thinking I reached out to touch the glossy
surface of one blue and gray wine jug.

The m'khashepah appeared on the other side of
the booth, a strange, red-purple samla covering her
thin body, her white hair smooth and anointed with
fragrant oil. She pointed at me. *The hand that works
the clay shapes the world.*

My fingertips touched the wine jug and it shattered, releasing a puff of white smoke and, oddly, a
familiar, cross-voiced complaint. *For what the mason
charges? I could build a new house.*

I snatched my hand away and looked over at
Amri's stall. It was empty, like all the others.

Wife you shall soon be, the m'khashepah said as she walked around the booth. *But whose?*

Alarmed, I tried to gather my wares, but every pot I touched disintegrated, releasing different colors of smoke and other, beloved voices:

These figs are too green, child. You shall give yourself a sour belly if you eat them.

I shall have to spend some extra hours at the wheel this night.

The dice were switched, and the last were weighted, I swear it.

The voices vanished, like the smoke, leaving me alone with the m'khashepah. The potsherds on the boards of the booth between us grew, the broken pieces multiplying and piling higher until I could only see her face, and she mine.

What will you do, Father's Delight? How will you keep them whole and safe?

I cannot do anything, I told her. *I am only a woman.*

Only a woman. She seized the last remaining intact pot and crushed it between her hands. White smoke enveloped her, and once more I heard Shomer's daughter say, *Devash is Noisan's only daughter, and she shall bring land and many sheep to her husband.*

I woke up with a cry, but I was not on my sleeping mat. I was at the center of the house, standing in front of my father's wheel. On the stone lay my striped head cloth, the one I never wore to market.

The head cloth of a young, unmarried betulah.

The m'khashepah's voice echoed inside my head. *When you doubt, go back to the wheel. Turn the wheel.*

I picked up my head cloth and held it in my hands. Now that I understood what could be made, I but had to find the courage to gather what was needed, and steadiness to shape it.

Taking care to keep my steps silent, I went to my parents' room.

CHAPTER

5

It was no more proper for an unmarried woman to travel alone between towns than it was for her to sell at market, but there were ways around such restrictions. Amri traveled to Maon every week to barter for goods with the trader caravans, and I knew the next morning was his day to go.

Just before dawn I slipped out of the house and met Amri outside his small dwelling on the edge of the quarter, where he was hitching his mule to his cart.

"Abigail." He seemed startled by my sudden appearance, until he saw the two-handled water jar at my hip. "I did not expect delivery today." His head went down and then up. "Why are you dressed like that?"

Beneath my mantle I wore my mother's best samla. Made of closely woven soft ivory wool with vivid blue and green stripes, it was the finest garment Chemda had ever worn, and smelled only faintly of the cedar chips she had sprinkled in its folds to repel

insects. I had never dared to touch it before; last night I had boldly stolen it from my parents' room while they slept.

"I have a favor to ask, Amri."

I thought of telling him that a sick friend had summoned me to Maon, but I was dressed too finely. I also needed the spice merchant to help me find Nabal once we arrived. In the end, it was simplest to tell him the truth, so I did.

"I would be in your debt," I added after relating the details of Rivai's debt and my solution. "If you will do this for me, anything I have to give is yours."

"I have enough pots, thank you, and your idiot brother should be whipped," Amri snapped.

"Abigail?"

I saw Rivai walking toward us and wanted to groan. "Brother, you should be home, sleeping."

My brother looked even worse than he had last night, his nose and mouth swollen and his eyes shot with tiny red veins. He moved carefully, too, as one did with an uncertain head or belly.

"I heard you leave." He looked from me to Amri and frowned. "What are you doing here?"

"I have asked Amri to take me with him to trade with the caravans," I told him. "I shall return this afternoon. Go home; Mother will be waking soon."

"You have no pottery with you," Rivai said. "Why are you wearing . . ." His expression darkened. "No, Abigail. I cannot permit you to do this."

"I was wrong." Amri folded his arms. "Your brother has some sense in his head."

"I mean what I say, Sister," Rivai said. "Our father will never allow it."

"I have done nothing yet," I reminded him, "nor is it likely I shall. But I must try."

"Child, how can you mean to throw yourself onto the mercy of a stranger, one who may be a cheat and a swindler?" Amri regarded my brother. "This ungrateful whelp is not worth it."

"He speaks the truth," Rivai chimed in. "Look."

He removed a small sack from his belt and opened it, revealing all the tiny carvings in bone and wood he had kept hoarded in his room. They were special to him, and I had only ever seen one or two.

"You see?" He closed the sack. "I shall go and sell these today at market."

My brother had never wished to sell his carvings, so it was apparent that he felt as desperate as I. But even if Rivai sold everything he possessed for three times its worth, it would not be enough.

"Let me see those, boy." When Rivai opened the sack again, the spice merchant inspected the collection of toggle pins, hair sticks, and ornaments. "They are pretty, but not worth more than one maneh of silver," he said, confirming my suspicions.

Rivai's eyes turned dull. "Then I shall go to the slavers. I am young, and strong."

"Selling yourself will only bring thirty sheqels." I looked at my feet, shod in my best sandals. "I must go to him."

"And what if this Nabal agrees to your bargain?

Do you think your brother will cease his drinking and gambling, and become a dutiful son?" Amri made it sound impossible.

I had not thought of that, and looked at Rivai. Tired and defeated, he was hanging his head. "If I can no longer live with our parents, will you care for them as I have, Brother?"

"Yes." He lifted his head. "I swear to you, I shall. And I shall never drink or gamble again." His eyes shifted to the horizon. "The sun will be up soon."

"So will our parents." I reached up and squeezed my brother's shoulder. "Go now. Say nothing of this to them until I have returned."

Rivai caught me in a tight embrace before he trudged away.

I had tried to sound brave, but I did not feel it. Indeed, I had to fight the urge to call him back.

"I shall see that he keeps that vow," Amri told me as he took the smallest pack from his cart. "Come inside, child. You will need more than that maiden's garb to make this scheme of yours work."

I followed Amri into his dwelling, which despite the rainwater damage to one wall, was larger and better built than my parents' house. Intricately woven reed mats covered the floor, while bunches of drying flowers and herbs hung from a wooden rack above my head. Stacks of filled baskets occupied each corner, except where part of the damaged wall had crumbled.

"You see?" Amri gestured toward the wood

planks covering one large, irregular hole in the wall. "Three sacks of millet the mason demands of me, and he works as a snail runs."

If only I had such troubles, I thought sadly. "Better grain than gold, my friend."

The spice merchant cleared his throat. "I complain too much." He placed the sack on his table and began sorting through it.

The spicy aromas of Amri's wares filled the room, particularly around another, narrow wooden table with an assortment of small querns and grinding stones. It was where he did his work, I saw, noting the traces of seeds and stalks on the saddle-shaped surface of the querns, and the jugs of oil and other liquids sitting to one side. There were also flat clay squares covered with triangular marks that I did not recognize at first.

"You can read and write?" I asked, astonished. I could not, nor could anyone in my family. Hardly anyone could but town scribes and high priests. Rivai had always wished to learn, but there was no money for a tutor or schooling.

"My father was a healer; he wished me to be the same and so taught me before he discovered the sight of blood made me ill. Here." Amri handed me a small goatskin vial, tightly bound with cord at the opening, and pointed to an open doorway. "Go in there and work this into the skin of your hands and face."

I loosened the cord and sniffed. The creamy-

looking liquid inside smelled of herbs and flowers, and something I couldn't identify. "What is this?"

"An old family recipe. Rub it in well." He walked to the entry door. "I shall return shortly."

Amri left before I could ask where he was going, and for a moment I feared he intended to go to speak to my father about my intention. There was a small but shameful part of me that almost wished he would. But through the front window, I saw him walk in the opposite direction of my parents' home. Wherever he was headed, it was not to expose me to my family.

I went into the small room, which was simply furnished as a bedchamber, and carefully applied the soft liquid to my face. The smell of the stuff was sweet and pungent, like a costly perfume, but it was too thin to be a proper ointment. It felt wonderful on my skin, however, and when I touched my cheek it seemed smoother and softer. I was startled to see that the rough, dry skin on my hands and fingers disappeared, too. It must have been a beauty lotion, like those used by wealthy women to keep their skin young and supple.

I had never been able to afford such a thing. When my skin became unbearably dry, I made do with a little goat's milk mixed with olive oil.

Amri had meant to help, but the fact was that I was not very young, or supple, or at all a wealthy woman. No beauty lotion in the world could change that, or make Nabal of Maon believe that.

What if I go all the way to Maon for nothing? My hands trembled as I adjusted the folds of my head cloth. *What if Nabal summons the shamar and has us driven out?*

In the wall above the sleeping mat on the floor, a section of brick had been chipped out to create a recess. There Amri had placed a small oil lamp, a libation saucer, and a polished bronze disk with edge notches that suggested the sun. Although idolatry was forbidden, such small shrines were common among Hebrews and gave comfort during the long dark hours of the night. The lamp's steady flame made the bronze gleam.

I knelt before it and bowed my head. "Adonai, since the days of Abraham, You have protected me and my people. You removed Egypt's yoke from our shoulders and brought us to this, the Promised Land. I beg You guide me now, so that I shall not lose my way, or my family." My throat hurt and my eyes stung. "What happens to me is not important. If You will only protect and deliver them, I shall gladly sing Your praises for all the days of my life."

"Abigail?" Amri called from the front room. "We should go now, before the sun rises."

A sense of peace filled me as I stood and wiped the tears from my face. "I am ready."

We rode in Amri's cart over the well-worn dirt road from Carmel to Maon. The journey took only a few minutes, but the spice merchant insisted I wear my head cloth with the end folds concealing the bottom half of my face.

"Do not show your features at any time while we are out-of-doors," he warned. "There are all manner of men here, and some cannot control their, ah, impulses."

I had never been to Maon, but sometimes on my walks I had seen the outside walls of the town from a respectable distance. More often I had spotted great flocks of sheep, during shearing time, being brought down from the mountains and driven to the gates.

Maon was larger than Carmel, but surely size was its only advantage, for it did not present itself as an attractive place in the least. The buildings and houses of the town had been built seemingly without order or plan, sprawled as they were around narrow, unkempt roads. Instead of building sewage gutters to carry away the refuse and animal waste from the streets, there were sanitary pits, which lay open to the air. Most were filled to overflowing with waste, and the troughs meant to drain them were cluttered with filth, providing an odorous fount for hordes of flies and other pests.

Why did the ruling men here permit this? Had our shofet discovered such filth anywhere within the walls of our town, he would have sent out the shamar to whip our citizens until they cleared it away.

From what little my father had said of Maon, I understood it to be a rough place, a man's town. I saw no women or girls about, and only male slaves at the communal wells. Odors seemed to hang in the air, particularly around the waste pits. Outside that stench, there was the strong smell of dung left behind

by countless herds driven, judging by the innumerable hoof marks, straight through the very streets.

"Does Nabal live here?" I asked Amri.

"There, at the top of that hill." He pointed to the largest building in sight.

My heart sank. Nabal must be very wealthy, to afford so much. His house offered a commanding view of the surrounding countryside, but a man who owned the largest herds in Judah would be expected to occupy such a lofty place.

How could this Maon be so rich and yet unmarried?

As we passed a man who lay unconscious and snoring by the side of the road, a flask of wine still clenched in his hand, the spice merchant glanced at me. "You have but to say, Abigail, and I shall turn the cart around and take you home."

I thought of my mother being brought here, to be sold on the auction block like one of his sheep. It would steal the rest of her mind and drive my father out of his. "No, Amri. I must see this man and do this thing."

"As you wish." He sighed and slapped the mule's haunch with the reins.

Nabal's property was extensive, and it took some minutes for the cart to reach the front of the house. I wondered if he was one of Maon's shofetim, for his home was built on a very large, grand scale, with hewn stone columns and plastered brick, almost like a small palace. The walls were painted with colorful

stripes, and fine screens of woven flax covered the windows. Carved wooden boxes hung suspended on either side of the door, the bright green fern and vivid flowers growing in them spilling over the sides.

Yet as Amri helped me down from the cart, I saw many signs of neglect to the outer properties, which appeared to belong to Nabal's farm workers. Weeds surrounded what were little more than shacks and tents, with only a few scrawny olive and fig trees. In contrast to the dense greenery around Nabal's house, the outer properties were obviously starved for water. As in town, mounds of dead leaves clogged the ditches providing drainage for the farmers, rendering them useless. Some water flowed in trickles here and there, but these only fed several stagnant pools fouled with green scum and tiny, writhing worms.

Nabal's animals, sleek and healthy-looking, occupied a pen to the side of the house. It looked as if he kept fifty sheep and as many goats for their milk and wool.

On the farmers' side of the fence, a few animals wandered. One lone, spindly-legged ewe came to the fence to peer at us. Dirt had turned her white wool gray, and her fat tail twitched listlessly against the cloud of black, stinging gnats following her. I thought her muzzle caked with mud, until I saw the dark blotches were actually dozens of ticks, hanging bloated with blood.

I had never seen such conditions. Not even the

poorest of the gerum by the beggars' gate lived like this. That anyone, even slaves, would be made to dwell in such squalor sickened me.

"Stay here by the cart," Amri said, his disgust plain. "I shall see if we may be permitted an audience." He straightened his turban as he strode up to the front of the house.

While I waited, I tried not to fiddle with my head cloth or mantle. I had only this first meeting to make a good impression, and I needed to be calm and collected.

Several minutes passed before the door to Nabal's house opened. After a short conversation with a servant, Amri nodded and returned to the cart.

"The master has not yet retired," he told me, "so he will receive us." He gave me a sharp look. "You are sure of this, Abigail?"

Afraid my voice would shake as much as my limbs, I nodded and took his arm.

CHAPTER

6

Being presented to the master of such a large house was a formal business in Carmel. Unmarried women were kept at home, and outside occasional visits to close female friends, not permitted under the roof of a stranger without a parent or chaperon. That was why I had needed Amri to accompany me, to keep my presence respectable and mannerly.

Here, however, manners seemed to have gone the way of the trees and animals. We were ushered in without ceremony and brought directly to a banquet room. The servant did not escort us in or announce our presence, and disappeared as soon as we passed over the threshold. I feared such an ungainly entrance might offend the master of the house, until I saw his surroundings.

It was clear that manners had not been of import here recently.

The remains of a large feast still lay on the tables,

beneath which skinny dogs slept among the discarded bones and scraps. When I saw two bare-breasted females, dressed in the abbreviated, semitransparent sadhin and standing on either side of a man sitting in a great chair, a startled gasp escaped me. Never had I seen women dressed so.

Amri followed my gaze and touched my arm. "Wealthy men keep bedchamber slaves," he murmured.

"Oh." I averted my eyes from their nakedness, feeling ashamed for them and embarrassed by my own presence, and looked instead at the man seated in the chair.

He was a large, bald man, and sat drinking from a goblet. He could not be called handsome or young, and indeed he seemed without much form, something of a lump of a man. Immediately I felt I was being unkind in my assessment, for he did possess regular features. Perhaps his eyes were on the small side, and set too close together, but they were a placid brown. His nose was neither too large nor too small, and only a little bulbous at the end. His skin and elaborately hemmed khiton were spotless.

If this was Nabal, he had his faults, but beyond them he appeared an ordinary man. Perhaps there was hope in that.

His extra chin disappeared as he regarded us, and his expression wavered between curiosity and suspicion. He made as if to speak, but the steward came in carrying two wooden tablets, and spoke in a whisper.

The man set aside his goblet to open the ivory-

hinged tablets, which possessed an inner, thick layer of wax upon which were writing marks. He listened as the steward muttered and pointed to different marks. At last he snapped the tablets together and shoved them at the servant.

"If I wanted the herds near town, I would have sent for them," he told the steward, his voice cross. "Nor will I travel to the hills to coddle them. They are paid to watch over my flocks, not to whine about marauders and hardships. Where is my hand basin?"

One of the female slaves offered him a small, flat bowl of water, in which he washed his hands. The other slave held out a towel.

"That I have used. Bring clean linen." He held his hands out to keep them from dripping on his fine garments and eyed us. "Well? What do you want?"

"We are grateful to you for seeing us," Amri said politely, free to speak now that we had been addressed. "You are Master Nabal?"

"I am. What of it?"

"I am Amri, spice merchant of Carmel." Amri bowed. "This is Abigail, daughter of the house of Oren."

"Oren. Oren." Wiping his hands on the fresh linen which the female slave had brought, he thought. "I know no such fellow."

"You gamed last night with his son, Rivai," Amri said. "It is his debt that brings us here."

The shiny brow furrowed again, and then Nabal uttered a grunt. "Nefat's friend. I remember him,

greedy for my gold he was. You have brought what he owes me?"

"I am the sister of Rivai, Master Nabal," I said, stepping forward and sinking to my knees before him.

Nabal looked me over with a scathing eye. "He does not owe me a woman."

Had he no mother, to teach him not to be so unmannerly to strangers? I had never been so insulted, yet I could not afford to offend him. "It is my brother's hope that I might please you."

"So that I shall say the debt satisfied?" He chuckled and threw out an arm, nearly hitting one of his slaves. "Were you ten herdsmen, or twenty comely maidens, I might be persuaded. But one slave is not worth eight maneh of gold."

"Were I a slave, that would be true, Master Nabal," I agreed as I rose. "But my brother does not wish to sell me. He offers me to be your wife."

It took some time for Nabal to stop laughing. As I stood in the face of his mirth, I thought of turning and running on foot all the way back to Carmel. I could not do this. I could not convince him to make Rivai's debt of eight gold maneh my bride price. Who would pay such an outrageous sum but shofetim expecting the loveliest of women in return?

I was not that. I was the unexceptional, the commonplace. Possessing neither name nor dowry, I was the daughter of a landless potter.

Truly I had never felt more worthless.

Amri came to stand beside me. "He seems the type to bargain," he said, only for my ears. "Make the most of it."

I did not want to take advantage of this unmannerly swindler, nor did I wish to pledge myself to him to erase Rivai's debt. I wanted to go home. I wanted my mother and my father. I was tired of being the strong one, the useful one. It was not fair to expect this of me.

No one demands this of you, the sharp voice of my conscience snapped. *You thought of this brilliant plan, and you made Amri bring you here. No one dragged you into it; no one even knows about it, do they? So cease your whining, and do your duty by your family.*

To save those I loved, I had no other choice.

In a sense, Amri was right: Arranging a marriage was no different than selling a pot. All I need do was convince Nabal of the bargain I was giving him. With steady hands I removed my veil and head cloth.

For once I had taken great pains with my appearance. I had brushed and anointed my hair, braiding the heavy length and coiling it atop my head, pinning it in place with two long picks Rivai had carved for me out of bone. There was little I could do to enhance the unremarkable set of my countenance—face paints were rare and expensive and, to some, a sign of questionable morals—but I had discreetly reddened my lips with pomegranate juice and used a bit of charcoal dust to darken my lashes and the rims of my eyelids.

I held my head high, as I imagined a queen would.

The beguiling scent of Amri's lotion still enveloped me, for Nabal stopped laughing and sniffed the air.

"That is a sweet smell." He examined my countenance. "I suppose you must wear it, for you are not beautiful, are you?"

So much for my homemade cosmetics.

"Young girls do not have the experience to run a household," I said, trying not to sound defensive. "Beautiful women are too busy attending to their looks."

"I do not need a wife or a housekeeper," Nabal said, "but you may beg me spare your brother." He made an expansive gesture. "Go ahead. I am in the mood to be entertained."

What did he expect me to do? Throw myself at his feet and cover them with kisses? My stomach clenched as I realized as his wife, I would be obliged to do just that, and anything else he commanded of me. I would have no respect or affection from this man.

Unless I demanded it.

"I would not deny you your pleasure, Master Nabal," I said, making my tone as sweet as honey, "but it is apparent that a match between us would not be agreeable on either side. My thanks for your consideration." I replaced my veil and turned to Amri. "We shall return to Carmel now."

Nabal's jaw sagged, creating another chin. "Do you imply that *I* am not good enough for *you*?"

"I would never presume to insult you so," I said.

"Then why do you go?" he demanded.

"I would not prove suitable as mistress of this place."

His brow furrowed. "Why not?"

Was he truly so addle-brained, or was it an act?

I took a moment to gaze about deliberately. "This house is acceptable, I suppose, but I saw animals outside covered in vermin. Your tenants live little better than beggars, and filth breeds disease." I let my nose wrinkle, ever so slightly.

"They live as they wish. I do not care as long as they do not step foot in here." Now Nabal sounded defensive and rather anxious. "What sort of disease?"

"Many kinds," I said, very matter-of-factly. "In any case, it is obvious that you prefer living without the interference of a caring wife. For that, and for intruding upon your time, I am sorry. Peace be upon you, Master."

Nabal sat up, outraged. "You *do* insult me."

"Then I may only ask your pardon again." I briskly adjusted my head cloth. "Come, Amri. There is no place for me here."

"Hold." Nabal rose from his chair, showing himself to be of average height, which only emphasized his softness and lack of form. His prominent belly swayed from side to side as he walked in a circle around us, inspecting me closely. "I would hear what makes *you* such a desirable wife, Abigail of Carmel."

"Many things." I waited until I had his full attention before I continued. "I would bring thrift and

industry to my husband's household. Slaves and servants cannot cheat me of a day's honest work, for I myself can cook, clean, spin, weave, and dye wool, as well as attend to all other domestic tasks. I have not been kept indoors all my days, either. For two years now, I have sold daily at Carmel market." I paused and took a deep breath, for I was about to admit what even Amri did not know. "What pottery I have sold there, I made with my own hands."

Nabal made a sound of disbelief. "Women are not potters."

"This one is," Amri told him. "She fashions the finest pottery in Judah, but she does not claim the work as her own. Her father is crippled, you see." He gave me an admiring look. "Not many daughters would be as mindful of their family's pride."

"I can see that," Nabal snapped. "She has all but rubbed my nose in her modesty."

"Her parents raised her well," Amri said softly. "Were I a younger man, I would take her above any other to wife."

"Fine, let us assume that she is, in truth, what you say." Nabal turned to me. "What zebed do you bring to a husband? Sheep? Goats? Land? How large is your portion of your father's nahalah?"

"I have . . . I bring . . ." I could not lie to him. There was nothing to be brought.

"This is the place?" a strident female voice called out. "By the Queen of Heaven, I have walked shorter distances to visit my relatives in the north."

"The steward says they are in here," another, familiar male voice said.

The door opened, and Shomer and Cetura entered the feasting room. The rug seller carried a heavy roll of colorful woven wool, while the grain seller's widow led four servants burdened with large, weighty sacks. Other merchants, similarly laden, followed them in.

"Why do they come?" I asked Amri in a whisper. I was terrified of seeing my father hobble in to demand I return home.

"I sent word to the other merchants." Amri smiled down at me. "Today the market comes to you." To Nabal, he said, "Here is the portion given to Abigail."

"A rug, fit for the king." Shomer dropped the roll of wool and shook it out, revealing the largest and most intricately dyed rug from his stall. He bowed to Nabal, and then came to me and took my hands in his. "For the madder root and the many other small gifts you have brought to me over the years." He squeezed my hands and then went back to his place.

"Four sacks of seed wheat, a full kor," Cetura called out to Nabal, directing his servants to place it next to the rug as she came forward. "Free of blight, mildew, and pests. Plant it anywhere and it will grow tall and golden as the sun." She, too, bowed and moved back to speak to me. "He is not much to look at," she said gruffly, and then bent forward to

kiss my cheek. "I would not know what a daughter's love is, but for you."

"Cetura." Afraid I would weep, I embraced her.

The other merchants stepped forward. Costly oils and foodstuffs were presented, as were fine wines and ales, artfully worked leathers and bronzes, rare resins and salts. Each merchant's offering I recognized as the finest wares they possessed. Each came to me and reminded me of some small thing I had done for them.

I knew what they were doing. I had no dowry, so they each had contributed something to create one for me. I wanted to cringe with shame. I wanted to sob with joy.

Geddel the clothes mender's offering made me gasp instead, for he brought a long khiton made of dazzling white linen. It had long sleeves fringed with fur and decorated all over with the tiniest of painted clay beads. So fine was it that I knew it had to belong to one of the wealthiest women in town.

"A samla as beautiful as its wearer," Geddel said gallantly, and after draping it carefully atop Cetura's grain sacks so that it would not become soiled, he walked to speak to me. "Tare, the shofet's concubine, did not want it back when she saw how dirty it was," he said in a low voice. "A fair trade for the basin, I thought."

I stared helplessly at the khiton. "But it is perfect." And worth ten times the wash basin I had given him.

"Not so. It is still a little damp from the hand

washing I gave it in your basin, after Tare left." He winked at me.

At last all the items had been presented, and the merchants formed a wall behind me and Amri. Nabal was examining everything with a greedy eye, muttering things to his hovering steward, before finally looking up with a frown. Like Amri with the juglets, he was wavering, but not yet convinced. But there was nothing else I could give, and I did not think offering to draw his water at the well would entice him.

His next words confirmed my fears. "This is it? This is all?"

The merchants exchanged unhappy glances. It was obvious to me that they had given all that they could spare.

"What would you have added, Master Nabal?" Amri asked.

"A bride's zebed is a permanent thing. Land or animals for the herd. Gold, like the debt her brother owes me." He smirked at me. "Your friends are generous, Abigail, but none of their offerings will last as long as a marriage. It is not enough."

"What more would you have the girl do?" Amri demanded, his face red with anger. "Go up into the hills and herd your sheep for you?"

I saw the steward's eyes widen and remembered the brief conversation Nabal had had with him earlier.

This is the filling for his water jug.

"I could see to the flocks." I knew nothing about shepherding, but I could learn. "It is a wife's duty to look after her husband's property, wherever and whatever it may be. Were you to take me there, I would—"

"I despise going into the hills," Nabal said. "All the women smell and look like goats, and the food and wine are disgusting. Every journey makes me ill for weeks. But if I do not go every spring, the herdsmen cheat me of my portion." He gave me a narrow look. "You say you would go there, in my place, as my wife. You would live alone, in the house I have in the hills of Paran. You would have to stay for all the months of spring, until shearing time."

The prospect utterly terrified me. "So I would, without complaint."

Nabal grunted. "The weaving and cheeses sent down to me have dwindled; that portion, too, must be increased. You would also see that I am not shorted ere the ewes drop any late lambs."

How could one be shorted of ewes? Or did he mean the tardy lambs?

Adonai, I hope I can learn all of this swiftly. "All that you wish would be done." He did not seem swayed, so I asked, "Your presence is required at once, is it not? I could leave after the wedding feast."

"So for this marriage I must also feed your kin and watch them drink up all my fine wines?" He shook his head.

Surrounded as we were by the remains of his feast from the night before, I felt a surge of impatience.

Was he so stingy that he would deny me a proper marriage ceremony?

That may be what he desires. Not only more water for his jug, but for me to fetch it.

"There need not be a feast, or any guests." I ignored Cetura's horrified gasp. "A holy priest to bless the union and issue the marriage contract would suffice."

It seemed everyone in the chamber held their breath as Nabal thought it over. I felt faint, my knees shaking under my khiton, but I would not collapse. I would show him the calm face of a capable woman who would make him a good partner and a strong and useful wife.

It seemed longer than it was before he spoke again.

"Very well," Nabal said, standing and puffing out his chest. "Abigail of Carmel, I shall take you to wife."

CHAPTER

7

"No," my father said that afternoon. "I forbid it. I *forbid* you to take this Maon as husband."

Amri had wanted to accompany me to the home of my parents, and give my father the news of my betrothal, but I refused. I knew it would be better for him to hear it privately, from my own lips. It was also the only way I could relate the details in such a way as to be pleasing to him.

I had expected surprise, and some displeasure, but not this dreadful anger.

"Father, it is done," I said as I removed my head cloth and sandals. "The agreement has been made. I go tomorrow to the house of Nabal to be married."

"I am head of this family, and you will not step foot outside this house without my say." My father's face spasmed with pain. "Impudent girl, I should beat you for daring to travel to Maon by yourself."

I ducked my head. "I was properly chaperoned."

My father didn't hear me. "Going to the house of

an unmarried man, flaunting yourself, accepting such an offer without kin beside you? Never have I heard of such scandalous behavior, even from the worst of harlots. How could you do such a thing, child? It is my duty to select a husband for you. This arrangement is invalid. It is illegal!"

It was many things, but it was not against the law. I had already consulted with Shomer on that. I had to be sure that no one could stop me. Not even my father.

"By entering Nabal's house as I did, I am considered betrothed. He agrees to marry me. It is done." I reached out to him, but he avoided my touch as if it were something foul. "It pains me that my choice has offended and upset you."

"It *pains* you?" He wrung one hand. "How do you think I feel, to know that my daughter steals her mother's clothes and paints her face? That she would steal away like a thief to throw herself at a Maon? Did you even consider for one moment the harm you have done to your family?"

I rubbed a hand over my reddened lips, trying to remove the stain. "It was wrong of me to act on my own, and I beg your forgiveness for my disrespectful behavior." I swallowed against the lump in my throat and held out my hand. "Please, Father, do not let this come between us. I am to be married. Be happy for me."

"Happy?" He stared at the red stain my mouth had left on my fingers. "Happy to know my daughter behaved like a veiled woman? To endure such

disgrace to our family name? To turn a blind eye to this unlawful betrothal?" He closed his eyes and shook his head.

I had to select my words carefully when it came to describing my betrothed. "Nabal is a very wealthy man. He has an enormous house in Maon, and owns the largest flocks in all of Judah." I waited, hopeful for a glimmer of approval. When none was shown, I added, "It is a good match. Far better than any I might have made here in Carmel."

"This match was not yours to make." Outrage burned in his filmy eyes, and for a moment, he was again the father of my childhood, tall and strong, and something he had never been before—terrifying. "I would rather see you dead than married to a Maon. You will send word of your refusal."

If I did not marry Nabal, much more than his love and regard for me would die. Now I had to do what I had never done: openly defy my father. "Forgive me, but I cannot do that."

He gave me a wide-eyed, shocked look. "You dare speak to me like this?" He lifted his crutch an inch, as if to strike me with the end of it.

"Yes, Father." I did not flinch away. "In this, I must."

"Tell him the truth, Abigail." My brother stepped into the room. He was pale and trembling, and the swelling in his face was still dreadful. But there was something else—something in his eyes—that made him seem different. "What she does, she does for you, and Mother, and me. Abigail acts as go'el."

"Nonsense. Women cannot be go'el, and no one marries but for . . ." My father's eyes became slits. "What have you to do with this, Rivai?" he asked in a very soft, dangerous voice.

"Nothing that cannot be mended," I rushed to say, but my brother cut me off.

"I gambled and lost to Nabal." Rivai glanced at me. "Abigail marries him to satisfy the debt. I tried to persuade her not, but she insisted she be my go'el."

If news of my betrothal had outraged Oren, my brother's confession shook him from his crown to his heels. He sagged and propped himself against the table with one hand. "How much is this debt of yours, my son?"

"Father, you do not understand, Rivai was cheated," I said quickly. "He was plied with wine and allowed to win so that he would become reckless. It is not his fault—"

"Silence, girl," my father said. His quiet voice was like a shout. "How much, Rivai?"

"Eight maneh of gold," my brother said quietly.

All the strength seemed to leave my father's body, and he sank down on the table bench. A dreadful moan died in his throat, and he covered his face with his hands.

"Why are you weeping, Oren?" My mother wandered into the room. "What is the matter? Did the goats knock over the oven shroud again?"

"No, all is well." I put an arm around her shoulders. "Come, Mother. We need to work in the garden."

I left Rivai to talk to our father and walked with Chemda out to where I grew my little patches of household herbs. I asked my mother to strip the seeds from the black cumin plants, which were so overgrown that she could not hurt them, while I thinned out the more delicate coriander.

I brought my hands to my face and breathed in deeply. The curly green leaves left their sweet-sharp scent on my fingers, a perfume I would likely not find in the hills.

"You are a pleasant-looking child." One thin arm stole around my shoulders. "What is your name, girl? My husband did not say."

The sickness that had sent Chemda's mind to bizarre fancies and meaningless wandering had also hurt me. From me, it had taken the mother who soothed my pains and fussed over my meals and combed out my hair. It stole the laughter and songs and love we had shared, and left me with this fragile, confused being who knew my name one day and forgot it the next.

She, too. I would leave tomorrow.

"I am Abigail," I told my mother as I moved out of her embrace and bent to pick up the basket of trimmings. "I am going away and I do not know when I shall return. You must stay close to Father now, for Rivai will be out working." But who would do the grinding and the cooking? Who would launder the garments and take the goats out to graze? Who would draw water and complete the thousand other tasks involved in keeping the family home?

Not my mother. My father would do what he could, but in the end the bulk of the work would be upon Rivai, who would also have to find some sort of work outside to earn enough to provide food for the family.

There would be no more time for his carving and dreaming. As useless as it was, part of me mourned that. Rivai may have been spoiled, but he did make his fancies into such lovely things.

"You should not worry yourself so." Chemda took the basket from me. "Let the men care for your troubles. That is why the Adonai puts them here."

The men had *created* all my troubles, but I could not tell her that. "I shall."

"Men cannot do everything." Cetura came into the garden and embraced me. To my mother, she said, "Chemda, would you have a cup of water for a thirsty old woman?"

I glanced toward the door but did not hear my father's or brother's voices any longer.

"Of course." My mother smiled; she liked Cetura. She wandered back into the house.

The widow inspected me closely. "You know nothing about herd animals."

I nodded. "I was desperate."

"Well, it is done, and you will have to marry that lout. I pray the hill people will be kind to you." She sighed. "If only you had not been too young for my sons, you would be my daughter in truth now."

"I am, in my heart," I assured her.

"Then as your other mother I think it my right to

see to the rest of the family after you go to your husband." She turned around. "My house is larger and more comfortable, I think."

I felt confused. "Cetura, what do you say?"

"I mean that your mother, father, and brother shall come to live with me. Since my sons went to Hebron, I have lived alone, and I am weary of it. I could use Rivai's strong young back to haul my barrows to market, too." She nodded in agreement with herself as she bent to inspect the black cumin. "I shall have to take a cutting of this; I have only the white, and these are sweeter. How many goats have you here?"

Something large and painful swelled beneath my breast. If Cetura took in my parents and brother, they would be well cared for, and never go hungry. Rivai would have work he could do. "You are jesting with me. You cannot do this. It is too much."

The widow eyed me. "I can do what I like, and when do you know me to jest?"

"Oh, Cetura." I flung myself into her arms.

"Child, child." She laughed and stroked my hair; then her movements stilled.

I lifted my head to see Rivai waiting with a cup of water.

Cetura murmured something about my mother and slipped into the house.

"I would do anything I can to make it right," Rivai said. "Anything, Abigail. Tell me and I shall, this moment."

"Cetura will look after you all when I am gone. She is getting older and needs a young man to do

the heavy work." I placed a hand on my brother's arm. "Promise you will do this, and help our dear neighbor in all things."

"I swear I shall."

"I love you, Brother. Never forget that." I pressed my lips to his cheek and went in. My father was watching Cetura and Chemda preparing the evening meal, but there was a terrible defeat in his eyes when he glanced at me.

"You return to Maon tomorrow, then?" he asked, as if he had never forbidden me to do so. "We shall come with you."

"No, Father." I could not tell him my husband was too cheap to provide a wedding feast. "The trip would be too much for Mother. Nabal sends me to the hill country directly, to look after his herds." I could not think about any of that now. "I do not know when I shall see you again. Likely not until after I return for shearing time."

"My daughter." My father's throat worked around the harsh rasp of his voice. "How can I permit you to do this? How will we go on without you?"

"Go as I shall, Father." I went to him and kissed his forehead. "With love in your heart."

Amri took me back to the house of Nabal the next day. Nothing had changed, and no one came to greet us. The steward admitted us and told us that the master was still in his private chamber.

"He stays in the baths until noon each day, perhaps a little later," the servant said.

I had never known anyone to take a full bath every day. My mother and I visited the public baths once each week but otherwise washed from a basin at home.

"Not this day," Amri snapped. "Wake him and tell him his bride is here."

"We will wait in the courtyard," I told the steward in a gentler voice. I wanted to see the garden, anyway.

We were brought to the center of the house, where the beds of rich soil, carefully tended, grew a bewildering variety of flowers. One small corner seemed neglected, however, and I went to investigate.

Absently I bent to tug at a melon vine, withered and dying. "These might have been saved," I said, fingering the tiny, neglected fruit.

"You would save everything," Amri said, his voice harsh, "but you cannot. I knew that witch in the market cursed you. She was the one to bring this misfortune into your life."

I glanced up at him. "How can a husband be a misfortune?"

"This man will be no husband to you." He drew me up and clasped my hands in a painful grip. "Heed me now, daughter of Oren. Herdsmen are nomads; they go wherever the flocks take them. They live in tents and have ways strange to you. Learn them. Their women will not be like you, and they will be suspicious of you. Befriend them."

The ferocity of his words startled me. "I shall try, Amri."

"Adonai yireh, but this is a bitter thing." He closed his eyes for a moment. "Where you go, you will have no friends or family to protect you." He looked at me now with the same, angry resentment the m'kha-shepah had shown me. "In all things, protect yourself. Save yourself."

The steward appeared before I could reply. He looked even more sullen and resentful. "Master Nabal will receive you now."

As before, we were brought to Nabal's great room. The air smelled of exotic spices, but none I recognized. Two male servants stood fanning Nabal with wide palm fronds. Another, older woman sat at his feet, into which she was rubbing oil.

My husband-to-be was naked to the waist and holding a round object with a handle in front of his mouth. He grimaced at the object and then applied a small, frayed-ended twig to his teeth.

Amri cleared his throat.

Nabal looked over the edge of the strange thing he was holding. "Why do you come here so early? Cannot this thing be done at night, when there is no sun to pierce my eyeballs or make me sweat?"

I did not know how to respond to that. I had never slept past the sun's rising in my life.

"It needs must be done now. Has the priest been summoned, and the contract writ?" Amri asked.

"Not yet." Nabal didn't seem overly concerned with the matter.

"I shall go to the bamot and bring the priest back." Amri gave him a hard look. "It will not take long."

"Whatever you wish." After the spice merchant had left, Nabal regarded me. "Why do you wear no jewels or ornaments?"

I did not wish to admit that I owned none. "I am not to have a wedding feast, so I dressed for a journey. You are sending me to the hill country today, are you not?" As beautiful as the house of Nabal was, I wanted nothing more than to be far away from this place.

He looked me over with a strange greediness in his eyes. "Perhaps I shall keep you here a day or two."

Before she had left last night, Cetura had taken me aside and in hushed tones told me of the intimate duties of a wife to her husband. The widow assured me that the pain I would feel at first would pass, and that in time it would grow to be a pleasant thing.

I looked at Nabal and tried to imagine part of his body inside my own in that bizarre fashion that Cetura had described in detail to me. It seemed a very unclean business, given the exact parts involved. I surely could not imagine my own parents doing such a thing. According to the widow, however, it was the only way to get children, and so I would submit.

I bowed my head. "As my husband wishes."

Nabal grunted and ordered one of the servants to bring wine. He then washed his hands and ordered the older woman to bathe his feet. Nothing was offered to me, not even a place where I might sit.

I turned to his steward. "Why has food not been brought? The priest will be here soon."

The steward blinked, confused.

"The priest comes to marry us, not to stuff his gullet," Nabal said. "He can feast when he returns to the bamot. The Adonai knows every year I am forced to donate enough food to that temple to choke ten mules."

I tried not to gape at him. Even as poor as my family was, we gave a portion of our food to the holy priests each winter. "Giving food to the bamot is to invite the Adonai's blessings upon your house, Master Nabal."

He gave me an unpleasant smile. "I have all the blessings I need."

Amri and the priest were ushered in by the steward a short time later.

"You are the daughter of Oren?" the priest asked. He was a tall, thin man whose imperious expression matched the grandeur of his finely embroidered linen simla.

"I am." I bowed over my open hands, the proper sign of respect for one who served the Adonai.

"This man had my scribe make up a contract, giving you to Master Nabal in marriage." The priest made this sound as if I was poised to run off a high cliff. "Do you agree to this willingly?"

I answered yes, and responded politely to the rest of his questions. It seemed as if the priest wished to persuade me out of the idea, but at last he sighed and made the sign of blessing over me.

"Let us see to this business, then, Abigail of Carmel."

Nabal did not take kindly to being rushed into the

marriage ceremony, and demanded that it wait until herbs could be brought for a sudden headache he was suffering. He also objected to the priest's suggestion that we stand together before him and instead had me come to the side of his chair so that he did not have to rise.

"Say your words over us, and bring me that contract, Priest," Nabal said, and gave me another of his oddly keen looks before drinking from the cup of herbs his steward had prepared.

I had only attended a few weddings, but they had been happy occasions in rooms crowded with the family and friends of the betrothed. Marriage was blessed by the Adonai, and brought children to renew the blood of the family. Brides were dressed with great care, draped in fine linen and gold collars, their skins rubbed with costly unguents, and their hands and feet tinted red to befit the crossing from maiden to wife.

Here in the house of Nabal, the priest's intonations sounded lifeless and hollow, echoing as they did within the nearly empty room. My husband-to-be seemed bored as he listened to the priest recite vows that would bind me to Nabal of Maon forever.

Each word burned into my heart like a flint brand. *You will take this woman to wife. You will give her home and children. You will protect her and keep her.*

Nabal did not wish to make such promises, that much was obvious. He snapped out his vows as if he resented being made to say them. He complained about a fly that happened into the room and stopped

the ceremony until one of the servants killed it. When the contract of marriage was brought for his mark, he made his mark at the bottom of the parchment too small, and had to make it a second time. He complained about that, too, and then had to have his hands washed again.

His behavior was atrocious, and so shameful my face remained red throughout the ceremony. By the time the priest was finished, I was full ready to weep, such was the embarrassment I felt.

The priest had far better manners and only showed a glimmer of distaste as he rolled up the contract and handed it to my husband's steward.

"Are we done?" Nabal demanded.

"Wait for the blessing," Amri snapped back at him.

"May the Adonai bless you with many sons, healthy herds, and fruitful pastures," he said as he waved a handful of seedpods over my head, and then Nabal's. "May you protect that which is yours. You belong to each other now, husband and wife."

Amri came forward to congratulate us, but he was very stiff and showed his dislike plainly. "You are a fortunate man, Master Nabal. I wish you receive all that you deserve."

I winced. His words were not exactly a blessing.

My new husband's upper lip curled. "May you have a double measure of what you wish for me."

The spice merchant turned to me. "Abigail, you are not to worry. Cetura will look after your kin."

I knew Cetura would see to my parents' comfort,

but that still left the problems with Rivai. Without strong guidance, he would surely fall in with the wrong sort again and put Cetura and my family at terrible risk.

"My brother could use some new friends. Someone who understands beauty, and can provide ways for him to sell his art. Perhaps a shrewd merchant who has no son of his own." I gazed up at him. "What do you think?"

The spice merchant said nothing for a long time, and then he muttered, "I think you could sell sand to one dying of thirst in the middle of the desert."

My mouth curved. "I was taught by the finest of teachers."

The steward came forward and led Amri from the room.

I was married, and my family was safe.

At last Nabal stirred and rose from his chair. The scent of the oil that slicked his chest and feet was almost overpowering, and his small eyes gleamed as his soft hand took my arm. "Come, wife."

Cetura had told me that husbands guided their new wives in their intimate duties, as most men had some experience with the matter.

"Be calm and quiet and do as he wishes," was her final advice. "Men know what is to be done, and he will likely make it quick for you."

I managed to hold my tongue as I went with Nabal to what I guessed was his sleeping chamber. It was nearly as large as my parents' entire house, but much

more richly furnished. The two bed slaves lay sleeping on the mound of pillows and furs that was apparently his bed. Their mouths hung wet and slack as they snored, and the thing responsible for their deep slumber—a large, empty wine jug—lay on its side between them.

"Lazy harlots." Nabal kicked the one nearer him, and she howled. "Get up."

The woman crawled over her companion to stagger, clutching her belly, from the room. Nabal simply started kicking the other until she, too, stumbled out in drunken haste.

"An Edomite gave them to me," my husband told me as he flopped in the middle of the mound and reclined. "I would sell them, but they have their talents. Remove that."

I reached for the wine jug.

"Not that. *That.*" He gestured toward my khiton.

Cetura had said there might be nakedness involved. I never disrobed, except when I went to the public baths, and that was done in the dimly lit bathing rooms with only my mother and other women about me. Now I would have to show Nabal what no one but perhaps my mother had seen.

Slowly I lifted the side edge of my khiton and brought it over my head. Beneath it laid only the shift I wore as an undergarment. I felt a bit ashamed at its threadbare condition, but I kept it clean and mended.

The sight of my shabby shift seemed to amuse my new husband. "That, too."

Ann Burton

I felt the full measure of a maiden's fear as I eased the shift off my shoulders and let it fall to my ankles. My face burned as if on fire, and I didn't know what to do with my hands.

Nabal looked at my pale, plump body, and shifted his gaze from my small breasts down to my round hips and back up again. "Unwind that braid."

I released my hair and drew the dark strands over my shoulders. Like other Hebrew maidens, I did not cut my hair, and unbound the curly ends nearly touched the floor.

The smile left Nabal's mouth, and he beckoned to me. "Come and lie with me, wife."

CHAPTER

8

I left for the hill country the next day, before dawn.
The journey would take until nightfall, Nabal's
house steward told me, and I would be accompanied
by four guards and an older serving woman. The
house in the hills that belonged to Nabal had not
been occupied for nearly a year, so provisions were
sent with us.

"You will go without delay, Mistress," the steward
told me when I came out of the small chamber ad-
joining my husband's. I was not given time to do
anything more than pack my belongings before I was
escorted out to the waiting wagon.

"Who are these men?" I did not recognize the two
men on horseback or the one driving the wagon, but
they carried many weapons: spears, knives, and
cudgels.

"Master Nabal's guards. They will escort you to
the herdsmen's encampment and return ere you are
installed there."

That would leave me with but a serving woman to put the house to rights before I summoned the herdsmen for the annual accounting—however one did that—and inspected the flocks. I did not dare demand anything; Nabal could easily divorce me for not fulfilling our marriage agreement.

"I would know the name of my husband's most trusted herdsman," I said with some desperation.

The steward gave me a blank look. "Master trusts no one, especially herdsmen, Mistress."

The serving woman, the one I had seen attending to Nabal's seat the day before, made an impatient sound from where she sat on the wagon's only bench seat.

"We have to go now, or we will not reach the encampment before darkness," she said in her gloomy voice. "If the bears and wolves do not attack us during the dark hours, the marauders will."

I had not thought the hill country so dangerous. Suddenly I felt glad the guards were well armed. "Why would marauders attack us?" I asked as I climbed up and sat beside her.

"For the mule, the horses, and the food. If we survived, they would sell us to slavers." The serving woman inspected me. "Have you never traveled through the hills?"

"No." I had never traveled anywhere.

"Good journey, Mistress," the steward said as he prepared to return to the house.

"Would you tell the master that I . . ." How did I

apologize for what had happened between us the day before? I had thought on it all night, but I was still not sure of what I had done wrong. "That I shall send word of how we fare?" I finished awkwardly.

The steward shrugged. "If you can, Mistress. If you cannot, he will send the men with fresh supplies in one moon."

One moon? I glanced at the pile of rations the wagon carried, which now looked rather pitiful. "Surely we will need them before then."

"The herdsmen have adequate for you." He gave me a pitying look before he called out to the guards. The one driving the cart slapped the reins on the backs of the two mules hitched to it.

With a jerk and a groan from the wheels, we were on our way.

I did not watch the house of Nabal disappear as the wagon lurched and jostled its way down the hill. I kept my back to it and looked over the horizon. If I squinted, I could just make out the top of Carmel's outermost wall. I wasn't sure, but I thought I could see the tops of the market stalls, too, and the smudge of smoke. Families would be rising now in the merchants' quarter, having their quick breakfast of bread and fruit before going out to sell their wares.

Right now Rivai is milking the goats, I thought, aching for the familiar sight and smells of my family's home. *Cetura will be grinding grain with my mother, and making tea for my father. Chemda will be so surprised when she sees the sweet rolls I made for her last night.*

Would my mother miss me? Or would her unreliable memories fade until I became forever a stranger to her?

"Here." The serving woman thrust something into my hand. A piece of dark bread, I saw, with a strange sticky cheese on one side. "Eat."

I nibbled at the edge of it, but the taste of the cheese was bitter, as if it were old. I did not wish to hurt her feelings, however, so I pretended to eat it while I dropped it, piece by piece, into my bag.

"That was unlike anything I've ever tasted," I said honestly. "My thanks."

She frowned at me. "You should not speak to me so. I am not a free woman. I serve you."

"I shall tell you a secret," I said, lowering my voice so that the driver did not hear me. "I have never before had a servant, so I shall probably say other things wrong."

The woman had eyes like a scale, ever weighing my words. After a long moment of silence, she said, "My name is Keseke."

It was not a Hebrew name, but it sounded familiar, as if I had heard someone speak a word like it once. "I am most grateful for the food, Keseke. It was thoughtful of you to provide it." I only hoped my stomach would not growl much during the remainder of the journey.

She glowered. "If you are to be our mistress, then you must do what is proper and stop thanking everyone for their service. Those who serve do so or they are starved or beaten."

Not by me. "Have you ever made this journey before? I understand my husband goes each spring."

"I have been to the hill country twice," Keseke continued, sounding even more aggrieved. "It is cold and empty. The house there is little more than a hovel."

Surely she exaggerated. Nabal would not live in such a grand house in one place and not in another. Then again, he did not like the hill country . . . perhaps she meant the house was simply smaller. "What are the people like?"

"The hill people? They live like the beasts." She gave me a long look before she added, "They harbor many hard feelings toward the master."

Did no one like my husband? I tugged at the edge of my head cloth.

Her gaze narrowed. "You did not have that bruise yesterday."

I tugged my head cloth forward so that it veiled the swollen, purplish mark on my cheek. "I was clumsy and fell."

"I know the mark of a man's hand when I see it." Keseke sniffed. "Too much wine, and you a maiden." She shook her head.

What had happened between my husband and me had been confusing, and I wished I knew Keseke well enough to ask her about it. But even were she my friend, it was not appropriate for a wife to discuss a husband with his—her—servant.

I would go into the hills with the mark of his anger on my face, for all to see. I did not understand why

Nabal had become so angry with me. Was it because I had known nothing about how to please him? I was a maiden; I was not supposed to know.

A day after my wedding, I was yet a maiden.

So I shall remain a maiden for a time, I told myself. *There is nothing I can do about it while Nabal and I are apart. When I return, I shall make a place for myself in his heart and his bed.*

I had to, or there would be no children.

"It is better this way," Keseke told me, as if she could hear my thoughts. "You do not wish to spend the months in the hills feeling sick and listless while your belly swells with child, do you?"

I shook my head. As badly as I wanted a child, I would not wish one now. My present burdens were large enough, and when time came for me to deliver, I wanted Cetura and my mother there to sing to my child, rub him with salt and cut his cord, and help me present him to his father.

Why was it so hard to imagine Nabal the father of my children?

"Well, then." Keseke made a face as the wagon's wheels bounced over a rut in the road. "My teeth will be rattled out of my head before we reach the crossroads."

"Where is this place?"

"In the valley, behind that peak." She pointed toward a distant hilltop. "The guards will stop there, and there is an old gerum couple who provide food and drink for passing travelers." She paused. "If they are still alive."

Did she mean the couple, or the travelers? I was afraid to ask.

It took two more hours to reach the valley of the crossroads, during which I checked own my teeth several times to assure they had not loosened. But the air was crisp and clean, and the sky a blue so bright and deep it almost hurt to look upon it.

What would it be like, to call these hills home? I was used to the crowded, merry noise of the market, or the sounds of busy families in our quarter. Here there was nothing that disturbed the stillness but the sound of the wagon and the horses. It felt unsettling at first, but as the time passed I thought I might easily grow accustomed to it. *This is how the world was before the Adonai made us. Simple and open and peaceful.*

Keseke did not speak much, but she readily identified different bushes and trees that I had never seen when I asked her about them.

"That is the juniper; the juice from its berries makes tough meat tender." She pointed to another, smaller patch of wide green shoots. "Look there. Those are leeks, as good as onions and garlic for flavoring."

"Were you raised in this part of Judah?" I asked her, curious as to how she had gained so much knowledge of the local plants and fruits.

"No." Her expression hardened, and she said no more after that.

By the time the wagon rumbled down into the valley of the crossroads, I felt bone-weary and in desperate need of a drink to clear the dust from my throat.

My stomach felt queasy, too. As the guards tended to the animals, Keseke and I climbed down and walked the path to the little house built in a grove of scraggly terebinth.

Before we reached the threshold, an old man emerged. He gave us a toothless smile as his dog, a friendly little thing with brown-and-white spotted fur, darted out to sniff at the hems of our samla. "You are welcome here, ladies. Come in and rest yourselves."

Nabal had kept the zebed the merchants had provided for me, and all I had to barter were some bone hair picks and amulets Rivai had made for me. Before I could retrieve them from the wrist bag I carried, Keseke produced a jar of fruit jelly.

"Green fig preserves," she told the old man. "Good for the digestion."

Inside the little house, an old woman sat hunched over a cooking pit, feeding bits of brushwood to the coals under a pot of bean stew. She wore no head cloth, and only a few twigs held her white hair in an untidy bundle at the back of her head. She barely spared us a glance as she set out bowls and bread on floor mats.

The dog went over to sit next to the bubbling cook pot, obviously waiting for a tidbit but too well-mannered to beg.

"Not many women travel the roads these days," the old man said, and I noticed his Hebrew was slightly accented. "Where do you go?"

"The hill country," I told him. "My husband sends me to see to his people and flocks there."

His face wrinkled. "Hard times now in the hills, it is said. The Philistines and the Amelkites have been raiding herds and burning villages." He glanced out the window. "It is good you are sent with guards. Your husband is a wise man."

Keseke interrupted by asking me, "Mistress, do you feel sick?"

"No, only tired. Why?"

"You did not eat much before," she said. "The jostling of the wagon will turn any stomach."

I assured her I was fine and in good appetite, which seemed to make her scowl all the more. The food the old couple provided was plain but filling, and their well water cool and clear.

As we ate, the dog came to my side and looked up at me. He would not beg, but there was such yearning in his bright, intelligent eyes. When Keseke went out to speak to the men, and no one else was looking, I fed him the bits of bread and cheese from my bag. He ate the whole, and then wandered over to the fire and lay down to sleep.

The old woman only nodded to my compliments as she served the guards, but her husband brought out some raisin and fig cakes.

"Take them with you," he said when I refused the treat. "We have more than enough, and they are good journey food."

"You are kind." I slipped two bone hair picks out

of my wrist bag and pressed them into his hand. "For your wife."

His rheumy eyes brightened. "These are worth more than a few fruit cakes, Mistress."

I shook my head. "They will keep the hair off her neck."

"I have already warned your men, but perhaps you should hear this as well." He looked at the guards, who were ignoring us. "Travelers who come here say that there are more than raiders in the hills. To the north, the king's men are searching for an outlaw. It is said he leads an army of runaway slaves and has single-handedly slain a giant. Many fear that this outlaw plans to attack the king and take over Israel and Judah."

I did not know of whom he spoke. "What has this to do with our journey?"

"There are rumors that this outlaw may have left the north to hide in Paran."

The story was an exciting one, for all the lack of detail, but I did not believe in giants or invincible outlaws. Still, I could indulge the old man's fancy. "I am glad, then, that it is not my task to stop him."

The journey from the crossroads to the herdsmen's encampment seemed to take much longer. Clouds spotted the serene sky with puffs of white and gray, and I wondered if it might storm before we reached the encampment. I would have to learn how to read the sky.

It did not help that I was peering into every stand of trees and cluster of bushes we passed. I did not know what I expected to see—piercing eyes, spears held ready to throw—but after hearing the old man's tale, I felt very uneasy.

Keseke's gloom deepened with every mile of road that passed under the wagon's wheels. She refused to share a cake of figs and only drank a little water from the skin the old man had refilled for us. She did, however, ask me if I felt sick with every passing mile.

"My belly feels fine," I told her. "Stop worrying."

After that, she did what she did well: complain.

"The air in the hills turns my skin to leather." She poked at her sunken cheek. "By the time we return to Maon, I shall resemble a lizard."

"Some goat curds mixed with oil will keep your skin supple," I advised.

"So I may smell of spoilt milk instead?" She *hmph*ed. "Then there will be the vermin."

"Vermin?"

"Rats, flies, snakes, fleas, ants," she listed with dismal delight. "If it bites or stings, I venture that you will find it in your bed or crawling down the collar of your khiton."

I looked out over the hills. "There cannot be that many, or the herdsmen would move the animals somewhere else."

"That is another thing." She shook a finger at me. "Don't touch any of the sheep, however clean they

look. They carry pests that will creep under your skin and into your hair. They feed on your blood and have to be burned out."

My mother had found some lice in my hair once when I was a little girl. She had smothered them with a liberal amount of olive oil. After that it had taken hours for her to comb out the eggs they had laid, but she hadn't burned me with anything. "I shall not go near them."

Keseke glared at the guards. "The Master should have left the men with us for the season. Women cannot be expected to drive off starving lions."

Rats and lice were bad enough, but now lions? I swallowed. "It will not be that bad, surely."

"What do you think carries off half the lambs each spring? And we two without protection," the serving woman said with a kind of relish, "for those lazy herdsmen cannot bestir themselves to look after their own women and children. They will do nothing but protect the sheep."

"Maybe we should take to wearing a fleece."

Keseke's nose elevated a disapproving notch. "Jest if you like, but it will not make these things go away."

She was right, of course. Women alone always had to be careful, particularly far from civilized places, and that wasn't a joking matter. I did not relish the thought of being snatched by marauders who would sell me to a slaver caravan—or worse.

"We should stay indoors at night, and only venture out together during the day." I might fashion a

staff for myself, too. Rivai and I had played Moses and Pharaoh with sticks when we were little, and I had nearly always won. A good club to the head might dissuade lions as well as slavers.

As long as I do not encounter that outlaw the old man mentioned, I amended. I would not wish to face a man whom someone as mighty as King Saul could not catch.

Keseke gave me a look of dislike. "Do you worry about anything, Mistress?"

So the serving woman did *not* know my thoughts.

"When this wagon will stop." I pressed a hand to the curve of my spine, which was now throbbing in time to the jostling of the wagon. "My back bones feel ready to split."

The wagon slowed but did not stop until we reached the edge of the wilderness. Valley pastures flowed wide and green at the base of the outer hills, which were dark with thick forests of oak and pine. In the distance, I saw a great flock of sheep move as one, drifting over and down a steep hill. There were faster, darker animals moving out the outside of the herd, and the faint sound of barking reached our ears.

"There it is." Keseke pointed at a small structure nestled back in a thick grove of trees.

In my eagerness, I did not wait for the wagon driver to help me down, but leapt from the wagon. I hurried to the grove, expecting to see servants emerge from the house and bid us welcome.

No one came out.

My steps slowed as I drew closer. Rotted boughs sagged over walls of cracked plaster and crumbling brick, while weeds and brush, blocking the dirt path to the doorway, grew as high as my waist. I nearly tripped over the door, which had fallen from its hinges and lay over the threshold.

Calling Nabal's hill house a hovel would be flattering it.

I peered inside. There were no lamps, no food laid out to welcome us. Perhaps my husband had not sent word that I was to come and stay. As I cautiously stepped over the fallen door, a nest of mice erupted from beneath it, squealing as they ran into several holes at the base of the house.

"We will need fire and water." Keseke came to stand beside me and eyed a dusty cobweb. "Keep your head covered or spiders will drop in your hair."

There was no danger of that. I was not going to remove my head cloth until I returned to Maon.

One of the guards carried a flint stone and, with a bit of grumbling, started a fire for us. The others unloaded the wagon. Keseke used the last of the daylight to collect brushwood to feed the fire. I tried not to look at the mess inside the house, but glancing up I saw patches of twilight sky through the gaps in the collapsing roof. The boughs supporting the reed mats under the roof plaster were rotted, and some appeared ready to drop at any moment.

"We cannot stay here," I told the driver of the wagon. "The house is not safe."

"You may see the herdsmen in the morning," the

driver said. "They can repair it." He sounded tired and grumpy, and revealed the reason for it with his next words. "We cannot, for Master Nabal ordered us to return tonight."

"But the animals must be exhausted."

He shook his head. "We change them at the crossroads." He handed me a sack half-filled with dried fruit. "This is the last of it. We will bring more supplies with the new moon." He went out to the empty wagon and climbed up behind the mules.

"Wait." I hurried after him. Part of me wanted to beg them to stay. Another wished to beg go with them. "Please ask my husband to send word to my family that I arrived here safely."

The driver nodded before he turned the mules and drove away, followed by the other two guards. I watched them until they disappeared over the rise, and then hugged myself with my arms. The setting of the sun brought coldness to the air, but it was the silence which sank into my flesh and gnawed at my bones.

"Well?" Keseke folded her arms.

Her prediction had come true. We were but two women in a strange place without adequate shelter, alone and friendless. The lions would likely come at any moment.

"It grows cold," I said. "Let us go inside and make the place livable for the night."

CHAPTER

9

Keseke proved very useful in finding things to make our new home somewhat more comfortable. She unearthed three unbroken saucer lamps and a juglet with a small measure of oil still inside. I made wicks for the lamps by twisting together threads plucked from the hem of my khiton, and lit them with a straw touched to a coal from the fire.

"There," I said as I set the lamps out. "We will have light by which to work."

A fallen pine branch worked nicely as a broom, and I used its stiff brown needles to sweep the floor while the serving woman banked the fire. She encircled the coals with stones and bits of brick, too, so that the fire would not wander while we slept.

"We should make some food now," I suggested, "while there is still enough oil to keep the lamps burning."

Keseke told me she would cook, but I insisted on sharing the work, so we both prepared the meal. Ke-

seke made a soup while I ground enough grain to make a small lehem to bake on a pit stone. The grinding stones were old and worn, and I spent a few minutes picking the largest pieces of grit from the flour.

Despite the present condition, this place had once been a permanent home for someone. "Who lived here before Nabal?" I asked.

"I do not know."

There were no bowls to be had, so we were obliged to share the pot between us. The hasty preparation and lack of proper seasoning did not seem important, as hungry as we were, and the hot soup proved to be tasty and filling.

"This is good," I told her as we dipped pieces of the unleavened bread into the broth. "What is it?"

"Food," was her reply.

Her terseness might have offended me, had I not recalled my husband's manner toward his servants. The woman had probably known little kindness from him. "I meant, how do you make it?"

"Leftover beans, a small onion, and a bit of marrow bone set to boil in water." She gave me a suspicious look. "Why?"

"I like it. I would make it myself, perhaps with some goat cheese crumbled atop it." Not that we had any cheese left, or a goat. I frowned. Would the herdsmen give us one of theirs for milk?

"Fennel improves it, too." The serving woman reached for the last heel of bread, hesitated, and broke it in half. "Here." She thrust one piece at me.

"What the master sent is not enough, but we can dig roots and greens. There are sycamore and nut trees here."

"My mother used to make me pistachio nut sweet cakes." The memory made my mouth water. "I wonder if there is any honey to be had."

"There are more important things to have first, such as a new roof," Keseke said. "If the wind does not cause this place to fall in on our heads before the morning."

"I shall pray it not." I gave her a rueful smile. "The driver said the herdsmen could see to it."

The serving woman sighed heavily. "Oh, they will, when they make time for it. Which could be tomorrow, or on the eve of the next moon, or the day after we depart for home."

"It does no harm to ask." If the herdsmen would not help us, then we would find the means to do it ourselves. I had taught myself to throw pots; mending a roof could not be much harder than that. "Where do the herdsmen camp?"

"I saw their tents over there." Keseke pointed to the east. "It is an hour's walk."

It was growing too dark to cross such a distance. "We shall go to them in the morning." I frowned and removed a bit of grit from my tongue. "Do you know any of these people?"

"The herdsmen?" The older woman sniffed. "Their names are too long and strange to recall. They do not let strangers see their women, only the master."

Just how aloof and unfriendly were these people? "I am the master's wife."

"I think you are too young to be let out of your mother's sight." She used a length of fallen wood to prop the door in place, and then wedged it in a clever way so that it blocked most of the wind. "I would not sleep on those mats tonight; they are likely full of bugs and mold."

I watched Keseke spread out her shawl to make a bed beside the cooking pit, and I did the same with my mantle. The dirt floor was cold and hard, and I shivered a little until the heat of the fire and the soup inside my belly warmed me. All at once weariness crept into my limbs, which felt as sore as if I had been carrying water back and forth from the well all day.

"I wake at dawn," Keseke said, as if to warn me. "Someone has to fetch water and wood."

"If you will do that, I can grind more grain and make our bread."

She gave me a sideways look. "If you wish to see the herdsmen tomorrow, I shall walk with you to the camp."

I hid a smile with my hand. "That would be pleasant." I did not have to pretend my yawn.

I was so weary I would have slept without dreaming, if not for the strange noises that kept assailing my ears. Owls called, insects chirped and hummed, and broken reed mats rattled as the wind chased itself through the remnants of the roof. Then there

were the growling sounds coming from the forest, the likes of which I had never heard.

There are lions and bears and wolves in this country, and we with no door to bolt and barely a roof over our heads.

Each time something woke me, I tried to identify the source of the sound. When I could not, I closed my eyes and murmured prayers to the Adonai.

Toward dawn, I woke to see a shadow hovering over me. "Adonai yireh."

Something thumped to the floor, and then Keseke crouched down beside me. "I thought I saw a rat crawling here." She shoved away the heavy branch she had dropped.

"I am blessed to have you here with me," I told her. "I shall praise the Adonai in your name."

"No more praise to Him, I beg you. Morning will come soon enough."

"I am sorry. I am a little afraid." I should have admonished her for speaking so to me, but I was shivering too hard. "And cold. Will you sleep beside me, so we can share our warmth?"

The serving woman stared at me in disbelief, and then rose, grabbed her shawl, and walked around the fire to lie beside me. "There, now. If anything comes in to attack us, it will feast on me first. Now go to sleep!"

"I shall." But not before I closed my eyes and sent a final, silent prayer of thanks to the Adonai for this new friend.

*   *   *

The next morning came far, far too early. It came with damp cold air, and thin light, and an ominous, rumbling sound that pressed in on my ears.

I sat up and gathered my mantle around me. My muscles ached from sleeping on the hard-packed dirt floor, but I forgot the soreness when another unearthly rumble filled the air. It did not fade away like the first, but seemed to roll around the house, coming from all directions at once.

"Who is there?" I called out.

Keseke rolled over, looked up, and groaned as she pulled a corner of her shawl over her face. "It is but thunder, Mistress. Go back to sleep."

"Thunder does not sound like that."

"It does here," she argued. "The valleys here carry its echo."

All my tiredness left me as I stood and went to look outside. The door fell out again the moment I removed the branch Keseke had wedged to keep it in place, and added to the lingering rumble with its own heavy thud. Outside, the air was as dark as inside the house, and swollen, dark gray clouds billowed up from behind the hills, rushing quickly toward the house.

My heart pounded as I stepped over the threshold and faced the storm. It was so close that it seemed if I reached out I might place my hand against the uneven, dark wall of clouds. At the same time, I had never seen the weather change so swiftly. The storm

raced toward the hill house like a charging army, pursuing the last bit of blue to the sky and swallowing it whole.

A different sort of movement caught my eye.

It came from a shepherd, who emerged from a thicket of trees and made his way through the swaying grasses and up the side of the tallest hill. The distance between us made it impossible to see his features, but from the way he moved I guessed him to be young and strong. He wore a mantle of blue over a plain ivory khiton.

Why was he climbing up there, in this weather?

At the very top of the hill, the shepherd fell to his knees and bowed his head. He remained thus for a few moments, and then rose and lifted his staff over his head. He seemed to be shouting something at the sky, but the rising wind snatched away his voice.

A crooked, white streak of light shot from sky to earth, so close to the shepherd that I covered my face with my hands. "No!"

When I dared look again, my hands fell to my sides. The lightning had not touched him, nor did he seem afraid of it, for he stood tall and straight and unflinching. Rain swept up and over the hill, pouring over the shepherd, who began to turn and twirl.

Slowly I walked forward, not stopping even when I felt the thunder shake the ground beneath my feet. Huge and terrible as the storm was, the man was not cowering or hiding or running way.

The shepherd was dancing. In the rain.

I had never seen anything so brave, or foolish, in

my life. I could not go back inside, even when the rain at last reached me. Instead I held out my arms as if to welcome it, turning up my face and closing my eyes.

In Carmel, the rain came soft and cool in gentle showers. Here, it was hard and cold and forceful, pricking my skin like a thousand tiny thorns. It was unlike anything I had ever felt, and my heart pounded in my breast. Now I understood exactly how the shepherd felt. How could one feel such power and not wish to shout and dance about for the joy of it?

"Mistress!" Keseke dragged me back to the house. "What are you doing? Have you no sense in your head?"

I laughed. "It is wonderful."

"It is rain. Wet and cold, as are you now." The serving woman guided me over to a dry spot under a part of the roof that had not fallen. She kept hold of me as she wiped my face with the edge of her head cloth. "You will catch your death of chill, and then the master will . . ." she faltered before she gave me an angry glare. "Never mind that. Hold still!"

She fussed at me until I removed my sodden khiton and changed into a dry one, and then built up the one fire the rain had not yet put out.

"This is a fine thing," she grumbled after we had shifted our supplies to a dry corner. "The brushwood is all wet and useless. We shall freeze."

Seeing the shepherd and feeling his exhilaration

were worth it. "Have you ever lived in such a beautiful, amazing place as this?"

Keseke's mouth sagged open. "Do you already have the fever?" She pressed her palm against my brow.

I laughed again and shook my head.

As swiftly as the storm came to us, so it went. A short time later the clouds had hurried on, and the sun came out, making every leaf and blade of grass sparkle. The air smelled fresh and alive, and I wanted nothing more than to run across the hills and breathe it all in.

"I want to take a walk," I told Keseke. I hoped I might see the dancing shepherd again.

"Good." The serving woman reached the door before I did. "We need dry wood, and reeds for new bed mats, and something to repair this roof before the beasts come to carry us off."

I looked over her shoulder and saw three men climbing up the hill. Was the rain dancer among them? "Perhaps we should first greet our visitors."

Keseke hissed at me to move inside, out of sight, but I covered my head and stepped out to meet the men, who stopped a few feet from the entrance to the house.

All three carried the long staff of the noqed, the keepers and raisers of herd animals. Living and working out-of-doors had tanned their skins to a deep, weathered brown, and they bore the scars and calluses of hard workers on their arms, hands, and

feet. None of them wore the blue mantle of the dancing shepherd.

Nabal's herdsmen.

Their dress seemed odd. The few noqed I had seen at market had the similar, roughly woven garments, but these men wore their simla shorter and without sleeves. Their sandals were plain leather soles attached to a single long strap that passed through a notch in their toes, encircled their ankles, and tied to a loop at the base of their heels. They wore no amulets or head coverings, and their beards were long and untrimmed.

The first and shortest of the men stepped forward ahead of the others. He had heavy, hooded eyes and the longest beard, with broad streaks of white in it. His two companions were younger men, darker and taller, but their features suggested that they were closely related to the eldest man.

They all smelled strongly of wet wool, sweat, and something that reminded me of milk when it soured.

I kept my expression polite and my voice respectful as I greeted the eldest of the trio. "I am Abigail, Zaqen. This is my companion, Keseke."

Keseke bobbed her head but said nothing.

"I am Rosh Yehud," the elder said, and used his staff to indicate the other two men. "My sons, Elas and Ur."

Rosh meant that Yehud was the leader and head man in this place. I was not certain if he was equal to a town's shofet, but I would treat him with the same deference.

"You are welcome at this house." I thought of the mess and standing puddles inside, and decided against inviting them in. "We have no drink or food prepared, but if you will spare us a moment we can bring—"

"Where is the Master Nabal?" Yehud asked. "We expected him to journey here for the yearly accounting, after the last of the night frosts, as he promised."

It became cold enough here for the ground to freeze? Would there be snow? "Nabal's business keeps him in Maon." I produced what I hoped was a reassuring smile. "He has sent me in his place."

My announcement took all three by surprise. Elas turned his head and made a soft, coughing noise to cover another, less polite sound. Ur simply stared at me with wide eyes.

Their father's stony countenance showed no change, but his shoulders stiffened, and his hand tightened on his staff until the gnarled knuckles turned white.

"This cannot be," Yehud said at last. "This is no place for a woman alone. You must be returned to your ba'al."

He thought me a slave and Nabal my owner. "The men who brought us here left last night, Rosh Yehud," I informed him carefully. "Nabal will not send them again until the next moon. We cannot do else but stay."

Elas choked and had to be pounded between the shoulder blades by his brother.

Yehud made a gesture. "Go back to camp, my sons. I shall join you there ere I deal with these women."

"But, Father—" Ur protested.

"Go." The quiet voice turned to flint. "Now."

I watched the two younger men trudge back down the hill and sensed a time of bargaining had arrived. I glanced at Keseke. "Would you fetch more water, please? We will need it for our meal."

The serving woman gave Yehud an uneasy look before she picked up a jar and walked off.

When she was out of earshot, Yehud stroked his beard. "You do not speak as a slave or servant would."

"I am not." I met his gaze proudly. "I am the wife of Nabal."

"If you lie to me, woman, you will have much regret in it." He inspected me. "When did the master wed you?"

"Yesterday." Before he could ask why I was not in Maon enjoying my marriage feast, I added, "My husband was quite eager for me to come to the hills and take the yearly accounting for him."

"The men of your family, they are to come here?" When I shook my head, he appeared confused. "Adonai yireh, why do they not?"

"My parents are too old and ill to make the journey," I said. "My brother is needed at home to care for them." Suddenly the hill country did not seem so beautiful, only far away from those I loved. "That is all the family I have."

"You mean to stay here with only that serving woman to attend you?"

"Keseke and I shall abide well on our own—"

The old man lifted his hand, a gesture so like Oren's that without thinking I fell silent. "Mistress Abigail, I have seven daughters of my own. They have lived in these hills since birth, and all are married and fine mothers to my grandchildren. Yet not one of them would I permit to wander about the land, or dwell by themselves. Not without protection. Either your father is dead, or he knows nothing of where your husband has sent you."

I was tempted to confide to the rosh the entire, wretched tale of my brother's debt. Yet if I was to deal fairly with these people, I would need their respect, not their pity.

"I am not your daughter, Rosh Yehud. I am your master's wife, and he sends me to do his work. That is what I shall do." I ignored the sudden contempt that glittered in his eyes. "I would appreciate your help with repairing this roof, and making this house habitable for me and my serving woman, but that is all I can accept on my husband's behalf."

"Your husband is a fool."

It was now apparent that my husband had very few admirers anywhere. Still, it would not do to allow such talk. "He is your master, and mine. I ask only what Nabal would ask of you."

"Then you are a greater fool than he." Yehud turned and made his way down the hill to where his sons waited.

I felt a familiar sense of frustration. Was my life to be a series of endless, impossible tasks, made all the more insurmountable by some man's ridiculous pride?

Stand and you shall fall, I heard the m'khashepah whisper inside my head. *Kneel and you shall rise.*

The only person who might help me in this place was walking away, deeply offended because I had tried to deal with him as a husband would.

"Rosh, please, wait," I called out as I hurried after Yehud. For a moment I thought he would not, and then he stopped walking and waited. I came to him and took a moment to catch my breath. "I was unmannerly and spoke in ignorance."

Yehud said nothing.

"You are right. I am but a foolish woman who has no family or friends in this place." I looked at the ground and tried to sound humble. "You advised me as a father might, out of concern. I see that now. Forgive me."

"It is good that your eyes have cleared." The rosh sighed. "Mistress, I cannot spare any of my sons to guard you or to take you back to Maon. Nabal's wife would not be welcome in our camp."

"Then I think you must leave me to live here, as my husband wishes." I looked out over the hills. "If I were to call your name from here, would you hear it down in your camp?"

"If you shouted it, perhaps." He glanced at the collapsing roof. "This house is not fit for a hoopoe, and it cannot be made right in a day and night."

I grimaced. "We shall be here longer than that."

He seemed to be deciding something again. "Very well, wife of Nabal. You and your companion may come to my camp tonight, and my wives will make you welcome."

It was the invitation I had hoped for. "I would be honored, Rosh Yehud."

CHAPTER
10

"I still do not see why we must bring food when we have so little for ourselves," Keseke grumbled that evening as we walked down the hill to the herdsmen's encampment.

"It is not polite to arrive somewhere empty-handed." I smiled down at the bundle of three lehem in my arms. Keseke and I had found a better quern stone near the house that afternoon, and the grain I had ground on it had turned to a fine, smooth flour. "Besides, that leek and root soup you made is delicious. Rosh Yehud's wives will enjoy it and praise your talent."

"Better *we* enjoy it ere we starve," the serving woman said. "Why do you keep looking about that way? Do you hear something?"

The twilight hid my blush. "No, nothing." Nor did I see any sign of the shepherd with the blue mantle, which disappointed me. "Their tents are very large, aren't they?" I asked as we passed between two of

the worn horoi stones, which Keseke had told me earlier marked Nabal's herd lands. "They must be comfortable here."

"For aimless wanderers." Keseke shifted the pot of soup she carried from one hip to the other. "Whatever they present to you, be it food, drink, or a gift, refuse it the first time it is offered, but accept it the second."

"Why?"

She glowered. "I do not know. It is their ridiculous custom, not mine."

That she did not wish me to embarrass myself touched my heart. "If you keep protecting me like this, I shall never become a terrible mistress."

"You already *are* a terrible mistress." The older woman's steps slowed, and her brow furrowed. "Now what is this?"

I followed her gaze and saw a group of men crossing our path. They wore the same garments as the noqed, but all of them carried spears and knives. One stopped long enough to look carefully at us before he continued on. "Perhaps they are Rosh Yehud's guards."

Keseke shook her head. "The herdsmen have never had guards."

We reached the outer tents of the encampment a few minutes later. The place seemed very strange to my eyes, accustomed as they were to seeing dwellings of brick and stone. Here the great tents of the herdsmen had been fashioned of goatskins, sewn together and stretched out over a frame of poles driven

into the ground. Ten or so tents formed a circle around a large cooking pit in the center, where a few women were tending to several pots nestled in the glowing red and black coals.

Naked children ran in and out of the tent flaps, exciting the dogs and scampering merrily about. They were completely ignored by their busy mothers. Only when one small boy tried to reach a dirty hand into a cook pot did one woman scold him. A moment later, she dipped a small bowl into the pot and handed it to him with a smile and a kiss to his brow.

"They allow their children to run free, the small beasts," Keseke told me. "They spoil them, too. They do not strike or beat them at all."

My parents had never raised a hand to me when I was a little girl, so I thought that a fine thing. I repeated one of Cetura's favorite sayings: "It is always easier to know how to raise another woman's child."

"Unless one is a slave," Keseke snapped. "Then one has no choice but to trot after the master's brats and wipe their bottoms."

I sighed. "When Nabal and I have children, dear friend, I shall attend to them myself."

She rolled her eyes. "So you say now. Wait until you have the little demons running about your household. Then we shall see how eager you are." She would have said more, but something seemed to make her start, and she fell into a silent brooding.

A young woman approached us. She wore a plain khiton and head covering like the other women, but

the tentative smile she gave us seemed friendly. "Greetings. I am Leha, daughter of Eulo, brother of Yehud."

It seemed a very formal greeting, but I returned it in kind. "My name is Abigail. I am daughter of Oren and wife of Nabal. This is Keseke, my companion and friend." The last word made the serving woman stiffen beside me.

"In the name of Yehud, my uncle, you are welcome here." Leha made a shy gesture. "Please, come with me."

We were led to one of the tents in the very center of the camp. The only way to enter was through a narrow flap, which Leha held open for us. Inside there were more than a dozen women sitting and talking, but their voices stilled as soon as we entered.

I felt very uncomfortable under the scrutiny of so many strange eyes. In the market, buyers never truly looked at me, only my pots. Here I was examined like a crack in the clay.

"I am neither friend nor companion to you," Keseke told me under her breath. "Why did you call me so?"

"That is how I regard you," I whispered back. "That is how you shall be called by me."

She muttered something that did not sound complimentary to my mother, but I pretended not to hear it.

"Aunt Bethel," Leha said, addressing an elderly woman, "I bring visitors." To me, she said, "This is Bethel, first wife of our rosh."

The white-haired woman rose but did not stand straight, and I realized that age had left her bow-backed. She showed no sign of pain, however, and regarded me with curious, bright black eyes.

I came forward to introduce myself and Keseke, and bowed with respect before I offered Bethel the bundle of lehem. "We are grateful for your hospitality."

"Wait until it has been offered," Bethel said in a voice as arid and ageless as desert sand.

Some of the women giggled, but Leha put a hand on her aunt's shoulder. "Aunt, please. Uncle invited these women here to meet us."

"Your Uncle is very fond of finding strays for me to attend." Bethel looked past me at Keseke. "Is that food you carry?"

"Yes." I placed the loaves on the mat where food and drink were laid out, and Keseke did the same with her pot of leek soup.

"You, I remember," Bethel said to the serving woman. "Is your tongue as sharp as it was last spring?"

"I cannot say." Keseke's mouth curled. "But it seems that yours has not changed."

"Age does that to a woman; that is why the Adonai makes old men grow deaf. In all things, there must be found balance." Bethel sighed and sat down again. "Come, take a place beside me, Abigail. Your mother should be proud, for your manners make up for your choice in husbands."

Bethel introduced each of Yehud's other four

wives, her and their daughters, daughters-in-law, nieces, granddaughters, and other assorted female relations, and although there were too many names for me to remember, many of their smiles were friendly.

The women here were not like those I knew well in town. A woman of Carmel who outlined her eyes with kohl would be considered daring, even foolish, for it was the practice of prostitutes to paint their faces. Yehud's daughters and wives not only darkened the rims of their eyes with the gleaming black cosmetic, but darkened their lips and rouged their cheeks, as well. The sweet tinkling of belled bangles chimed from their wrists and ankles, and silver and gold rings glittered from pierced earlobes.

"They jingle like harlots," Keseke muttered next to my ear.

"I like the sound," I said, earning another glare. "It does no harm to wear such out here, away from strangers." I imagined Yehud and his sons appreciated the care their women took in making themselves attractive.

Bethel invited us to kneel by a wide mat filled with bowls and platters of food, where she said a blessing over the meal.

Leha offered us steaming hot cups of a pungent herb tea. I remembered to politely refuse the first offer and accept the second, and won an approving nod from Bethel. I was too anxious to eat much, however, and that, too, was noticed.

"You peck like a bird." Bethel shook a finger under my nose. "Up here the nights are cold even into sum-

mer, and without a husband to keep you warm you will need more flesh on your bones."

She had given me a generous helping of grain softened in a strong-flavored meat broth. It was unfamiliar to my tongue, but I tried to swallow a little more. "How long have you and your family dwelled here, Bethel?"

"More years than I can count," she said. "My mother's grandfather and his kin came here from the land bordering Egypt and farmed for some years before they became herders for the master's family. Yehud's kin came here from the east when my mother was a girl."

"So you grew up together." The thought charmed me.

"Women grow up. Men grow beards." She cackled out a laugh.

Leha offered me a small bowl of lumpy white liquid. The smell identified it at once, but I still asked, "Is the milk, uh, soured?"

"Curdled. We drink it so. It is called leban. Try it," she urged.

I could not pinch my nostrils closed and pour it down my throat—that would have been rude—but I confess, I did hold my breath. The taste was as sour as I expected, but the coolness of the milk and soft curds slid easily down my throat. If not for the oddness of the leban's taste I might have called it refreshing.

The meal finished with a generous offering of fig cakes and sweet grapes. Keseke and I were the object

of all eyes, and whenever I spoke, some of the women covered their mouths with their fingers and murmured to each other behind them.

"Stop that," Bethel said when one of the younger wives sitting closest to us indulged in such whispering. "Where are your manners?" She scanned the faces around us. "All of you, behave yourselves." To me, she said, "They wonder why your father wed you to such a mean-spirited man, who would send you far into the wilderness only a day after your wedding, as if you were gerusa."

Gerusa were what Hebrews called a few poor women in town, women to whom my mother had never allowed me to speak. When I grew older, Cetura explained that the gerusa were outcasts, divorced by their husbands and left to fend for themselves. It was something that generally did not happen the day after the wedding.

"I do not yet know my husband very well," I admitted, "but it was not his displeasure or cruelty that sent me here. I freely offered to come in Nabal's place and do the accounting."

"You see?" Bethel gave one of her daughters-in-law a haughty look before she gestured to me. "No tears, no petty grievances aired. She does not bleat like a shofar blown to the wind. This is how a proper wife speaks of her husband."

I could not remember the name of the daughter-in-law she reproved, but the younger woman's expression darkened, and she rose unsteadily. As she

stalked out of the tent, I saw the unmistakable curve of her belly under her loose khiton.

"When is her child due?" I asked.

"Within the moon, if it comes out at all," Bethel said. "That babe has had to listen to his mother Malme wail and cry for months, and I fear it will not wish to be born in a world of such noise."

"Aunt, that is not fair," Leha said in her gentle voice. "Malme has never been away from her mother. Our ways are still strange to her."

"No stranger than hers, which are evidently to lie about all day, fret, and refuse to work." Bethel shook her head. "I told Irev not to marry a Jezreelitess; women from the cities want too much attention." Bethel gave me a sideways look. "Well, perhaps not all."

"Carmel can hardly be called a city." Gratefully I handed Leha my empty food bowl and refused more of the leban.

"Tell us a story, Leha," one of the children begged, and the others chimed in until Bethel's niece smiled and held up her hands.

"I shall, but only one," Leha warned, "and then it will be time for sleep."

Bethel chuckled as the children groaned over this. "They would have Leha spinning her tales until dawn."

The children gathered closer to Leha as she began to tell her story.

"This tale is of a terrible soldier from Gath, a cruel

and boastful man who stood six cubits and a span. He was of the Rephaim, a tall and arrogant people from the west who take gold to make war on Israel and Judah.''

I had heard rumors of the mercenary Rephaim, who were often hired by the Philistines to serve in their army. Nothing good had ever been said about them, and they were so large that many Hebrews thought them a race of giants.

Letha leaned forward, moving her hands expressively as she described the monster. ''He was the champion of the Philistine army, and towered head and shoulders above the very tallest men in all the lands. So, too, this giant was unnaturally strong, for he walked about wearing a coat of copper mail that weighed as much as five thousand sheqels, and wielded a mighty sword with a copper blade that weighed six hundred sheqels.'' Her voice dropped to a menacing whisper. ''His very name caused dread and fear in the hearts of brave men, so people only whispered it, as do I now, for he was Goliath, the Giant of Gath.''

I saw Keseke's eyes widen like the children's, and suppressed a smile.

''Now, it was known that the Philistines wished to make war against good King Saul and Israel, and so they brought their men into our land and took up on one side of the valley of Ephesdammim. Our brave king sent his army to face them, and as the battle lines were drawn, the enemy sent out their

dreaded champion, Goliath, to strike fear into the heart of Israel.

" 'I come to challenge your greatest warrior,' Goliath cried out to the Hebrew soldiers. His voice was like thunder, and shook the earth under their feet. 'Send out one man to fight me alone,' said the monster, swinging his battle sword over his head. 'The loser of this combat shall cause his army to surrender, and henceforth they shall become as servants to the army of the victor.' "

"That's not fair!" one boy cried out.

"That is what you get when you trifle with Philistines," Bethel said, her voice stern but her eyes twinkling.

"What happened next, Leha?" the boy demanded.

"Well, day and night for forty days, Goliath stood and called out his challenge to the army of King Saul, but no soldier dared accept it. For who would risk an entire army on the outcome of a fight with such a monster who would surely win against anyone who stood up to him? And so the Philistines laughed and taunted our army, and our soldiers felt the bitterness of defeat and shame." Leha held up one hand. "Such it was, until a shepherd came into the camp of the Hebrew soldiers. Although he carried no sword or spear, and wore only a simple khiton, the young shepherd boldly strode to the edge of the valley and summoned the brute Goliath. The shepherd was David, warrior son of Jesse."

The children gasped.

"David had heard of Goliath's challenge and had journeyed all the way from Bethlehem to face the monster. And so the giant emerged from the Philistine's camp, his towering body clad in his polished coat, a spear in his left hand, and his great copper sword in his right. Before him walked his armor-bearer, carrying a long javelin of iron and an enormous shield. As Goliath came to face David, every Hebrew who saw him fell and covered his head and trembled with fear."

"But not Melekh David!" someone cried out.

"The Giant of Gath called upon the gods of the Rephaim to shower David with stones from the sky and bolts of lightning and other evils," Leha said. "He would show the Hebrews that their Adonai was no match for his many, powerful gods."

"That was silly," one girl said. "There are no other gods but the One and True."

Leha nodded. "But Goliath did not believe in the Adonai, nor in the shepherd who had come in His name. The giant ridiculed David, trying to shame him into retreating. Then David spoke, and his voice rang out over the valley."

Leha paused, waiting until the children clamored for more before continuing with the tale.

"This is what David said: 'You have come to me with a sword, and a spear, and a javelin, and a bearer laden with a shield. But I come to you with the name of the Lord of our armies, the One and True, the Adonai of Israel. It is He whom you have taunted with your boastful words.' "

"Did he try to kill David?" a small girl asked, her eyes huge.

"No, little one. As Goliath lifted his sword to strike at David, the shepherd slung a single stone from his sling, the only weapon he carried. The stone struck the giant in the center of his brow, and he fell to the earth. David then went to stand upon Goliath, and used the giant's own mighty sword to cut off his head."

The bloodthirsty children cheered.

"After the great battle that followed this, David took Goliath's head to Jerusalem and left it there for all who doubted the might of the Adonai to see. Then he returned to tend to his father's herds in Bethlehem."

"As a good son should." Bethel clapped her hands together. "It is time for sleep, children."

"Bethel, when we came here we saw some armed men walking along the edge of your camp. Has there been some sort of trouble for the herdsmen, that they are needed?"

Bethel gave Leha a strange look before she answered me. "Those dal are not our men, nor should they be here."

Dal, those who had fallen from prosperity, were usually beggars—not armed men. I thought of the tales the old man at the crossroads had told me. Surely the outlaw giant-killer he had mentioned was not David, but these dal might very well be his army. "Are they threatening you?"

"No, not us." She waved an impatient hand. "If

you wish to know more about the dal, you will have to ask Yehud, for it is none of my doing."

"I see." I doubted the rosh would appreciate my questioning him. "This morning I think I saw one of your sons upon a hilltop near my husband's house. He did not appear at all afraid of the storm."

"Any son of mine has the sense to take cover during a storm," Bethel said, now puzzled. "What was he doing up there?"

I could not describe his fearlessness in the face of the storm, or his dancing. I did not want her—or anyone—to laugh at him. "I am not sure. The man carried a staff and wore a blue mantle."

All the friendliness left Bethel's face. "I do not know of whom you speak, but a wife newly wed should not be watching strange men walking the hills alone. Stay away from the dal, too. Leha." With the help of her niece, she struggled to her feet. "It grows late. You will stay here for the night."

CHAPTER
11

Rosh Yehud's wife Bethel insisted Keseke and I stay in camp until her sons could repair the roof of the hill house. Storms came each afternoon and lasted far into the night, so it was only sensible to abide with them. There were so many women that the tents were crowded, but they were also warm and dry.

My serving woman had no real objections. "Everything smells of goat and sheep, but there is enough to eat, I suppose, and men to watch over us." She gave me a stern look. "You are not to be alone with any of the men. Most of them are married."

"So am I, and I do not wish to be." That was almost true. I did think often about meeting the shepherd who had danced in the rain. It was a childish wish, and nothing could come of it, but still my thoughts lingered on him.

I looked for the blue of his mantle whenever I walked outside the tents, but saw no sign of him.

The few women I asked about the shepherd did not seem to know of whom I spoke.

I began to think I imagined him.

The armed men we had seen the first night appeared now and then, but they never spoke to any of us or moved within the camp. Most often I saw the dal patrolling beyond the torches, circling in groups of five and six, always alert and carrying many weapons. I had no opportunity to ask Yehud about them, for the rosh left at dawn with the herds and did not return until late at night, when he retired to his tent and sent for Bethel or one of his other wives to attend him.

"My uncle is having some trouble with other herdsmen from the south," Leha told me. "There is only one stream where the men can water the herds at the noon hour, and sometimes our men are made to hold back the herd and wait while the southerners water their flocks. Since ours are much larger than theirs, and our sheep are thirsty, the men must work hard to keep them back."

"Is the water on my husband's land?" That would mean our herdsmen deserved the right to use it first.

"No. It cuts through land that belongs to King Saul." Leha made a face. "The king's law says whoever comes first, waters first."

With each day, I learned a little more about the way Yehud and his people lived, and the difficulties and hardships of tending the flocks. Each morning the sheep were brought out of a walled pasture, which Leha called the sheepfold, at the edge of camp.

The flock was so large that it had to be divided, else the sheep were in danger of scattering and being lost once up in the hills.

Yehud's sons all had their own portion of the flock to drive to graze, and incredibly each had trained his sheep to come at the sound of his voice. I would not have believed it, had I not watched three thousand sheep divide themselves as they came out of the sheepfold and follow their herdsmen in smaller flocks.

"Sheep are not as witless as one might think," Bethel said. "The ewes protect their lambs, even from their own shepherds. The sound of a stranger's voice will make the entire flock turn and flee."

After learning that, I took care to be very silent whenever I was near the sheep. Leha noticed and laughed at me. "They will not run away unless you use your voice while trying to herd them."

I looked out over the sea of white fleece in the sheepfold enclosure. "I do not think I shall try that."

The herdsmen did not carry a great deal as they and their dogs drove the sheep to graze. Each morning Bethel and the other women prepared leather food pouches with bread, fig cakes, and olives for the men to take with them for their midday meal. Besides the pouches, which they carried slung over their shoulders, the herdsmen carried long wooden staffs, some soft pieces of hide, and vials of olive oil.

"The hide is for bandaging any legs the sheep might injure," Leha explained when I asked her about the unusual items being packed in the shep-

herds' bags. "The oil is rubbed on open wounds to slow bleeding and cover the scent of blood, which attracts beasts."

There were many hardships to be faced. Forever at the mercy of the weather, the herdsmen endured the heat of summer and the cold of winter as they made their daily drives. Lambs too young, weak, or weary to make the journey from camp to graze or back again had to be carried like children. When they felt threatened, ewes giving suck could unexpectedly turn and butt and kick, and their hooves often inflicted deep gashes.

Even after the day's work was finished, and the sheep were counted and safely contained within the sheepfold, one man took a turn as doorkeeper. That meant standing guard at the entrance to the pasture, staying awake through the night, and driving away any beasts that tried to attack the flock.

After driving the sheep up into the hills to graze and drink at the stream, the herdsmen had to turn their flocks around and drive them back to camp, hopefully before dark. Once there, each man counted his sheep as they passed under his staff and into the sheepfold. Then the doorkeeper for the night would stand guard until dawn, when the whole process had to be repeated again.

It was a hard life, but a good one, too, I thought. The herdsmen trained their dogs well and displayed a rough sort of affection for their herding partners. They often brought back some fruit, berries, or herbs they found while out with the sheep, and directed

the women as to the source so they could go gathering. One husband brought a handful of wildflowers for his blushing wife, while another produced a wooden ring he had whittled out of smooth, hard oak for his young son, who was fretting with sore gums.

I grew to love the people as dearly as I had the merchants in Carmel.

Leha, Bethel's youngest niece, quickly accepted my offer to help with the daily chores of grinding, cooking, milking the goats, and looking after the youngest of the herdsmen's children. I did not mind the work, and preferred to keep busy so that there was no resentment at my continued presence in the camp.

Leha in turn did much to ease my way among the other women and particularly liked to hear stories about life in Carmel and selling pottery at market.

"We can weave the baskets and clothing we need, but we must trade for our pots," Leha told me. "There is plenty of clay near the crooked hill path, but we have no potter."

I asked her to show me the place and found the dark, reddish clay to be thicker and stiffer than that near the springs of Carmel. I dug out enough to make a few things and demonstrated the hand-roll method of making simple pots and bowls, which could be fired in the camp's large stone bread ovens.

Leha was skeptical, until the first firing cooled and I presented her with a shallow serving bowl and two cooking pots. "These are wonderful, Abigail."

I had made no slip for the pottery, and they lacked

the perfection of balance and form that wheel turning gave the clay, so I did not share her enthusiasm. "Likely you could trade for something prettier, but they will serve."

"Pretty things do not last very long, and so we do not have much use for them. Whatever we can produce ourselves saves us that much in trade." Leha gave me a rueful look. "We are a plain, dull people, I fear. It must be much nicer to live in town with all the conveniences."

"It is more convenient, but not better." I had grown to love being in the camp, surrounded by the women and children. "I have always wondered what it would be like to belong to a big family. I envy you. At home I only have my brother and my parents."

"And your husband and his kin," Leha reminded me.

Yes, there was Nabal. The husband I had left behind, and of whom I rarely thought now. As I watched the herdsmen's children chasing each other through the labyrinth of the tents, I wondered what would happen to me when I returned to his house. *We will have many babies, and caring for them and Nabal will be my life.*

Bethel was so delighted by the pottery I had made that I promised to share the method of fashioning the pieces with Leha.

"My husband will be pleased by what you have done," Bethel told me one night after the evening meal. "When he returns, I shall ask him if you may stay the summer here with us."

The prospect delighted me, until I remembered what I was supposed to be doing for my husband. "I think I had better not. Bethel, when my husband came here last spring, what did he do?"

"Besides drinking all our wine and eating all our meat?" She made a sound of contempt. "He slept all day, had our women haul a thousand jugs of water to his house, and made my husband and sons very angry with his constant complaining."

I cringed a little. "No, what I mean is, what did he do for the yearly accounting?"

"He ordered the herds counted, divided for shearing, and then figured our portion." She eyed me. "You have done this? You know how our portion is reckoned?"

I could no longer keep up a pretense, not with her. "No. In truth, I know nothing about herding or the accounting of it."

"Yet you offered to come here and perform these tasks." Bethel made a clucking sound with her tongue. "What were you thinking, girl?"

"I thought I might find someone who could instruct me." I gave her a hopeful look.

Bethel laughed. "Such an innocent face, for one so devious. Now, now, do not take offense, girl. I suspect that you have your reasons for coming here, and I like your spirit. You fooled a man none of us like, and you have given us the gift of your skill with the clay. I shall be happy to teach you what is to be done with the herds. Does that suit you?"

This trade was more than fair. "Yes."

*   *   *

The next day Keseke and I returned to the hill house, which now had a sound roof. The inside was damp from rain, but with the longer, hotter days would soon dry out. It took two days to clean and set the place to rights, and I missed the company of Bethel and the other women, but given their unhappiness with my husband, I did not wish to impose on them any longer.

Keseke reverted to her former gloom. "I had just grown used to sleeping in those smelly tents."

"I can borrow one from Rosh Yehud and pitch it outside, if you like," I teased her.

After our morning chores were finished, I walked down to the camp to spend a few hours making pots with Leha and the other women. The first results were somewhat hilarious—even hand-rolling clay requires some skill—but my students were nothing if not determined. Within days the women of the camp began producing clumsy but usable pottery, and I assured them that with time and practice, their work would improve.

Bethel kept her word and taught me how the annual accounting was done. The previous year's count was kept on wooden disks, notched one time for twenty animals counted, and dotted for single animals. My task was to count the animals under Yehud's care and make two new sets of disks, one for the rosh and the other for my husband. From these I learned that Nabal owned over three thousand sheep and a thousand goats.

"So many," I said as I stacked the disks and replaced them. "I did not know."

"These are the animals that were lost after shearing." Bethel gave me a single disk with black marks counting nineteen animals. "They are to be taken out of Yehud's portion."

Yehud's portion was only one sheep out of every fifty and one goat out of every hundred I counted. That was his only pay for the entire year, so a debt of nineteen animals would lower his portion considerably. "How were they lost?"

The old woman eyed the black-marked disk. "A few died of sickness. Most were stolen by marauders during the night, when Yehud has the fewest guards around the sheep."

I was confused by this. "But there are so many dal patrolling the encampment each night." Indeed, when I passed them after dark, they seemed like a moving wall between the camp and the rest of the world.

"I told you, those men are not ours. They—" Bethel cut her words off. "It does not matter. The dal were not here last season."

"I see." I didn't, but it was plain that she did not wish to speak of them. "In any case, it does not seem right that Rosh Yehud should suffer the loss of stolen animals alone. Why does my husband not take half from his own portion?"

Bethel gave me a sharp look, but then claimed she was tired and the teaching would have to wait until the next afternoon.

Keseke accompanied me to the camp every day and spent her time watching the children while I taught pot making, until the morning she stepped into a burrow hole while she was out gathering wood.

"I shall get a stick to use as a crutch," she told me, her face ashen with pain as I applied a warm poultice of barley mash and aromatic oil to her badly wrenched ankle. "There is no need to pamper me. I am your servant."

"Yes, you are, so you will stay here and rest," I said. "I mean what I say, Keseke. If you move an inch, I shall beat you."

She snorted. "You cannot bring yourself to kill spiders."

"They eat the other insects. I do not see you doing that." I finished wrapping her ankle and stood. "You are not to do anything while you sit, either. We have plenty of water drawn and flour made, and I shall collect the figs from the drying rack ere I return."

"The water is stale, and those figs will need another day in the sun," she claimed. "You need not go to the camp today."

Maybe she was lonely. "Do you wish me to stay with you?"

"I am fine." She scowled. "But you should not walk down alone. What if you come upon a wolf or a bear?"

"I was more hoping to meet one of those lions you told me of." I picked up the stout length of oak that I had taken to carrying with me wherever I walked.

"We could cure the pelt and have a nice rug to spread before the fire."

Keseke made an annoyed gesture, waving me away. "Go on, then. You will not be happy until you are beset by a beast."

"I shall fetch some fresh water first." I grinned. "And if I am met by a lion at the spring, I shall tell it that I was a fool for not following your advice before it devours me."

Of wolves and bears and lions, I saw nothing, but indeed I was beginning to feel much at home in the hills. Everything was so open, and green. Birds sang and chattered and chirped all day, and when the sun set, the crickets took up the chorus. At other times the only sound one could hear was a lovely whispering from the wind as it wove its way through the pines.

The spring lay near the edge of the trees behind the house. Small, and partially hidden by an outcropping of weather-scoured rock, it was a bountiful source of cool, clear water. I followed the narrow path, formed by years of bare feet treading back and forth.

I must ask Leha if she has a piece of leather I may have to make a soft splint, I thought as I stepped through the gap in the stones. *Keseke will not be able to walk without something around that ankle.*

The sun was already hot overhead, so I removed my head cloth and loosened the collar fold of my khiton. Keseke often predicted that I would be as dusky as a Nubian if I did not keep covered up, but

the sun's warmth felt good on my hair and neck. I smiled and shook out my hair before a splash made me stop in my tracks.

Someone was already at the water's edge, drawing up a brimming pail with a long wooden staff: a man, bare-chested and wearing only a leather ezor around his hips. A traveling pack of food lay spread on the stone beside him. He sat back, poured the water over his head, and shook like a dog before he began singing in a deep, melodic voice:

Adonai, Adonai,
How excellent is Your name in all the earth,
Who have set Your glory above the heavens!
Out of the mouth of babes and nursing infants
You have ordained strength,
Because of Your enemies,
That You may silence the enemy and the avenger.
When I consider Your heavens, the work of Your
  fingers,
The moon and the stars, which You have ordained,
What is man that You are mindful of him,
And the son of man that You visit him?
For You have made him a little lower than the angels,
And You have crowned him with glory and honor.
You have made him to have dominion over the works
  of Your hands;
You have put all things under his feet,
All sheep and oxen—
Even the beasts of the field,
The birds of the air,
And the fish of the sea

That pass through the paths of the seas.
Adonai, Adonai,
How excellent is Your name in all the earth!

As he finished the lovely song, I stepped back, but my foot dislodged a stone and made a small sound. Before I could blink, the man had risen, turned, and held the staff as if he meant to strike me.

"What do you want?" he demanded, his beautiful voice now fierce and flat.

A marauder. I froze. "Water." I held out my empty pot to show him.

Slowly the staff lowered. "Only water?"

"Nothing more." I averted my gaze from his bare chest, which was dripping with water, and spotted a wet cloth near his feet. Obviously he had been using the spring to wash and rest. "I did not mean to startle you, Rea."

"Did you like my song?"

"It was wondrous," I said. "I have never heard anything the like."

He nodded. "If it pleases you, then I shall not change the words."

"The song is your own? But how—" I remembered I was talking to a nearly naked, wet man and my face grew hot. "I do not mean to intrude. I shall wait beyond the stones until you are finished."

"No." His voice gentled. "I am done here." He bent to pick up his simla and shrugged into it. "This water is almost as sweet as that I drank as a boy, from the cistern at my town's front gate."

"Sweet water is a good thing. To find, and to drink." Oh, why had the Adonai stricken my tongue with such clumsiness?

I pressed back against the stone, but I could not stop watching him. He was not very tall, only perhaps a head taller than me, but his shoulders were unusually wide and his arms brutally heavy with muscle. Years of back-breaking work could carve a man's body so, but he sang like one who had spent his entire life doing nothing else but idling by springs and praising the Adonai.

Who was he? One of the dal?

He moved with a peculiar sort of ease, though, one that reminded me of something that I could not quite recall. I was sure I had never seen him before, so why did he seem so familiar?

Like a starling's feathers, his wet hair was straight and shiny, and of black so deep that the light brought glints of blue from it. His brows and beard grew just as dark, although his beard was very short, as if just growing in again after being shaved. The shaving of it meant that he had recently known the death of a relative or friend. His skin seemed cast of smooth bronze. Even if he never sang a note, wherever he went, women's eyes would follow him.

I sensed something different about him, something that had nothing to do with his handsome face, nor his garments, which were as humble as any shepherd's. He wore no ornaments or belt, and his weapons were no different than those carried by a common shamar. Perhaps it was his long-lidded

black eyes, as exotic as obsidian beads, bright with intelligence and humor, and yet calm and deep as the cool water from a mountain well.

A shepherd, a warrior, a singer, and a poet. How could a man be all those things at the same time?

He glanced at me. "You are staring at me."

I was. Being caught at it made me wish I could run to the spring, dive in and sink to the very bottom, and stay there until he had forgotten that I existed.

"I am sorry." I moved to leave, but the breeze caught my hair and flung a handful of it into my face. I set down the water jug I carried and tried to brush it from my eyes.

"Wait." He moved so quickly that the space between us was gone before I realized it. Large hands slid along cheeks and lifted the curtain of hair from my eyes. "Ah, there you are hiding."

I could not move. The stone was at my back; he at my front. I felt as if caught between two immovable forces, and then nearly laughed at myself for my silly thoughts. *How can a man be as strong as stone?*

He was not made of stone. He stood so close I could feel the heat of his skin through my khiton.

That reminded me of my place, which was not to be this close to him. "My thanks." I tried to draw to the side, but he moved to stop me.

"Don't run away so quick, shy one."

"I am not shy." I would not duck my head again, or let my lashes flutter. I would *not*.

"Then why have your cheeks gone a pretty pink, little dove?" He smoothed my wayward hair back

from my brow, and took the head cloth from my numb fingers. Like a father would for a young daughter, he draped my hair and folded the ends of the head cloth around my neck. "It is good that you keep your tresses covered."

Did he think my hair so ugly? I felt stricken by the thought.

"I shall. It was just that the sun felt so nice, and I . . ." I was beginning to babble. "I shall keep it. Covered, I mean."

"It is only right. Such bright and lovely hair should be saved for your husband's enjoyment." He did not remove his hands from my face, but tilted it up to examine it. "Your skin is too pale for you to be one of Yehud's women. What is your name, and where are your kin?"

Who was I, to be allowing this man to put his hands on me?

"Abigail." I would have added, "wife of Nabal," but that part did not wish to leave my tongue. Guilt piled atop my embarrassment, but I could not make the words come out. Indeed, my throat was so dry that breathing was a chore.

"Abigail, Father's Delight." He nodded. "It is a name befitting one with such gentle eyes. Where is your bet ab?"

"The house of my father is in Carmel, beyond the hills." I pointed vaguely in that direction. Or perhaps I pointed to Hebron. With my thoughts so muddled, I could not tell east from west, north from south.

His dark brows rose. "You are very far from home, little dove."

"Are you?" I dared to ask.

"Unhappily, yes. My journey here was not of my choosing, but perhaps soon I shall be permitted to return." His eyes went to the horizon, and he seemed to forget my presence. "This strangeness of his will pass, as it always does. It must."

His words were so heavy with sadness that I wanted to embrace him. I gripped the sides of my khiton with my hands to resist the urge. "I shall keep you in my prayers."

"Your kindness warms a cold heart." He looked over my head. "Now I must go."

I turned to see three of the dal from Yehud's camp waiting just beyond the stones. "Oh. Of course, I shall not keep you."

The man reached to take a bundle of cloth from a flat-topped stone. It was a mantle spun of light blue wool, the same one I had seen on the mysterious man on the hill.

"I saw you face the lightning, the other day," I blurted out. "You stood atop the hill. You danced in the rain."

He smiled a little. "Do you do nothing but follow me about?"

I was mortified. "I did not mean to spy on you. I just . . . saw you. It was the first time."

"But not the last. Someday I shall sing and dance for you again, little dove. But for now, I must work."

He tucked one last, stray piece of hair under the edge of my head cloth. "We will meet again."

We could not, for I was married. Yet before I could say as much, the man went to join the other dal.

I stared after them until they disappeared beyond the trees, and only then did I realize that I still did not know his name. Who was he? Why was Bethel afraid of him and the other dal? Why did the dal carry so many weapons, for that matter, and why did they guard the camp so closely? Was Yehud their rosh?

My heart did not care about any of that. My heart was making a knot of itself. *Will he truly sing and dance for me someday, as he promised?*

The turmoil in my head was nothing compared to that in my heart. I felt dizzy and weak and excited, all at once. I wanted to drop everything and run after the man, and learn his name, and speak with him about his homeland and why he had come to Judah. I wanted to soothe the frown from his brow and spin stories to make him laugh. I wanted to hear him and talk to him and listen to more of his songs and be with him—

No, that was not all.

I wanted to put my hands on his shoulders, and stroke my palms down the length of his arms. I wanted to press my mouth to his. I wanted to feel his hands in my hair and his breath on my face. I wanted to hear him call me his little dove again, in the darkness as the two of us lay together in the

sweet grass, with the sky and the stars as our tent, and the night air as our only garments.

I wanted to be different for him, to be made different by him. I wanted him to shape me with his touch, paint me with his kisses, and fire me in the kiln of our hearts, beating together.

Hot tears scalded my cheeks. I wanted *him*. But I was not free to want any man except the one to whom I was wed.

I slid down the stone and rested my cheek against my knees. I felt hot and cold all over and trembled as if I had fever.

"Adonai, Adonai." I lifted my watery gaze to the sky. "What have I done?"

CHAPTER
12

I did not tell Bethel or Leha about the man I had met at the spring, or about my shameful behavior. I did not think of being wed to one man and wishing to touch and be naked with another. It was a sin simply to think of such things. Hebrew women of remote villages were still stoned to death for committing adultery. Even if an adulteress were only cast out and divorced by her husband, she could never return to her family.

That I would never allow to happen.

I did not understand why the shepherd had made me feel such desire. I had not felt such with my husband, but I had not done my duty by him. I brooded over it until Keseke made mention of my mood.

"What is wrong with your tongue?" she demanded as we were out gathering wild wheat stalks in a field by the camp one afternoon.

"Nothing." I ignored the displeasure on her face and tugged a thick, yellow-green stalk from the

earth. Leha had showed me how to roast the wild wheat's seed heads over an open fire, which made them brown and crunchy. The children especially loved them as a treat.

"You do nothing but chatter all the time," the serving woman said, coming to take the stalks from my hand and add them to her basket. "Now I hear not two words from you in an hour. You have not been puking, so I know you have no babe in your belly."

My cheeks turned to fire. "No." I reached for another stalk. "I am not with child." I stopped and glanced at her. "You were married once, were you not?"

The corners of her mouth turned down. "I was."

"Was your duty to your husband . . ." How did I ask why Nabal and my shepherd had treated me so differently? "Was it always pleasant? Did it make you happy?"

"Not always, but yes." Keseke dropped the basket at my feet and planted her hands on her hips. "What did he do to you?"

"I do not know what you mean."

"The master. He took you to bed, and the next morning you had a bruise on your face. What happened between you?"

Reluctantly, and with great embarrassment, I told her. The duty had not been a pleasant thing. The feel of Nabal's plump, oily flesh on mine had made me shudder. "He did not kiss my mouth, but he did pinch and fondle me a great deal," I said. None of that had been gentle. "Then there was that other business."

"What other business?"

"My friend Cetura had told me that Nabal had to put himself inside me. I lay beneath him and let him where he needed to be"—I swallowed—"but something was wrong, and he could not. I think I am not made as other women."

"I have seen you make your water," Keseke said dryly. "You are just as any woman is. Why could he not come inside you? Were you too narrow?"

"No." I tried to think of how to describe it. "His part was so small and soft I thought it would go in without difficulty."

The serving woman stared at me for a long moment, and then she began to laugh. She laughed so hard that she fell to the ground and rolled on it.

"Very well." Humiliated, I snatched up the basket and started to walk back to camp.

"Mistress, wait. Wait!" Keseke caught up with me and made me stop. "I was not laughing at you, girl. It was the master at fault, not you. His part must be long and stiff and hard to go into you."

"Oh." I frowned. "But what did he wish me to do about it? He kept saying for me to do something in words I did not know, and when I did not, he hit me and made me leave his chamber."

Keseke put her arm through mine and looked around until she spotted a shade tree. "Come, sit with me. I shall explain it to you."

I listened to everything she said and felt my unease fade as she told me of Nabal's difficulty and how

other men suffered such an affliction from time to time.

"Well, what did he expect me to do about it?" I demanded. "It was his part, not mine."

The serving woman described some ways in which women could make that part of men long and stiff enough for the business of making a child. It involved much kissing and fondling of a kind that I did not think I might have done, even if Nabal had allowed such contact.

"Cetura told me only to be quiet and obedient," I said firmly. "I did ask him for direction, you know, just before he knocked me away with a fist and blamed me for it. He said he had no desire for me and that I should send his bed slaves to him."

"So what did you do?"

"What else was I to do?" I threw up my hands. "I told the steward to send the Edomites to Nabal and to show me to a separate chamber."

Keseke laughed again, but not nearly so long or loud. "Mistress, you were not at fault. The master has always had difficulty even with his bed slaves. Such failures strike at a man's pride." She smiled as if the thought of this pleased her.

No wonder he had been angry. "How am I to get children of him, then, if we cannot do this thing?"

The question made her go still for a moment before her sour expression returned. "It is getting late now. We should take these seed heads back to camp and roast them for the children."

* * *

Shearing season was only a few weeks hence, and so I applied myself to the accounting and pot making. I would show Nabal that his faith in me was not misplaced, and give him no reason to cast me off. I pushed aside thoughts of the shepherd.

Nothing I did would shame my husband or my family.

Working among the herdsmen's women in the camp helped keep my thoughts from straying in unseemly directions. Perhaps that was why I began to see things I had not before.

The sheep and goats had used up most of the graze surrounding the camp, and the herdsmen were obliged to drive them farther away each day. Food stores that had seemed plentiful needed constant replenishing, and with the uncertain weather, daily gathering was not always possible. The shepherds from the south competed for local game, which grew scarce, and the grain sacks began to empty rapidly. The growing heat and lack of graze caused the goats' milk to dwindle, and the children would beg their mothers in vain for a cup of leban or a piece of cheese.

With all this bounty my husband possessed, Yehud's family were barely surviving, and they would not receive their pay for the year until shearing time.

Nabal's men returned at the new moon as they had promised, and after I shared the meager amount of food they had brought with the women of the camp, I decided to make the trip back to Maon.

Keseke predicted my efforts would result in nothing but failure. "The master will not care what you say. He will send nothing for these people, and he will beat you for nagging him on it. It is better you stay here."

"Yehud and his sons cannot herd the sheep if they are too thin and weak from lack of good food." I finished making up my pack of garments and food for the journey. "I have asked Leha if you may stay in the camp until I return. The women will take care of you."

"I do not need their coddling." She scowled at her swollen ankle. "I serve you."

"They will take care of you," I repeated, bending down and pressing a kiss against her thin cheek. "Behave yourself while I am gone."

She seized my hand in hers. "Mistress, do not go back to Maon. Stay." She gestured around us. "Does the house not please you? Are we not comfortable and happy here?"

"We are, and that makes it all the more important I go." At her blank look, I added, "How can I live like this when Yehud and his people go hungry?"

"The master will do terrible things to you," she muttered. "He will beat you."

"Nabal is my husband, Keseke. He can beat me any time he wishes, but I think he knows not to make waste of a good wife." Her expression filled with fear so swiftly that I became concerned. "What has he ever done to make you so frightened of him?"

"Nothing." She would not look at me.

"Then you must trust me to—"

"Listen to me." She seized my shoulder in a painful grip. "It is said that the master was not to inherit the nahalah of his family. He had an older brother, Pela, who was to have the land, the family holdings, and control of their wealth."

Servants always gossiped about their masters, but I was surprised she knew so much. "What has this to do with my return to Maon?"

"Pela was murdered, as were the master's parents. On their mats, as they slept. The master was only a young boy, ten years old, and the only one who survived the night. He told the shofet that he saw brigands come into the house in the middle of the night." Keseke swallowed. "Some think he killed his family, so that he would have everything to himself."

"That is ridiculous." I would have laughed, had the tale not been so gruesome. "A boy of ten cannot kill three adults."

I hardly heard what she said next, her voice dwindled so low. "Perhaps he found someone else to do the killing for him."

Whatever Nabal had done to her, it had twisted her mind. I was tempted to take her back to Maon with me, but given the wild tales she was spouting, Nabal might order her whipped or sold.

"Enough of this," I told her. "I am going now. I wish you to stay in the camp while I am gone. Do you understand?"

She nodded and stared at her hands.

"I shall return soon." I kissed the top of her head and walked out to the wagon.

The journey back from Paran seemed to take longer, now that I traveled alone in the back of the wagon. The driver and the guards had not been happy about taking me back with them and seemed disgruntled over my presence. When we stopped at the crossroads to have a meal and change the animals, the driver said one of the wagon's wheels was loose and that we would stay the night so that the men could repair it.

The old man seemed pleased to see me and had no trouble offering me a sleeping mat by his fire for the night. The men he sent to the barn, where there would be room for them to work and sleep.

"We thought you would not return, Mistress," the old man said as he brought me a bowl of soup and some bread.

"It is earlier than I had planned, but I have need to see my husband and family." I smiled at the old man's wife, who was as quiet as ever but wore Rivai's carved picks in the tidy roll of her hair. "Where is your dog?" I had expected to see him sitting and trying not to beg by the cook pot.

"He died one night," the old man told me. "From the signs of it, he must have eaten something that disagreed with him." He smiled sadly. "After first we met, I heard your servant speak of your illness, and worried you might not fare well with it in the mountains. That is why your return surprised me."

I frowned. "But I am not ill, nor was I when last we came here."

"That cannot be right. She told one of your men that she expected your family to hold kispu before the new moon." He grimaced. "My ears are old. Doubtless I heard wrong."

Kispu was a ritual only performed after someone died, and I had never been in better health. Why would Keseke predict such a horrid thing for me?

The old woman came over and looked at me. "That night after you left was when our dog died," she said, her voice shy. "I think the Adonai must have sent your sickness into him, to spare you."

We left before dawn the next morning and reached Maon by midday.

The house of Nabal looked exactly as it had the day I had left it, with the addition of a few more tick-ridden animals wandering around the slaves' quarters and deposited dung ere they roamed. My husband's steward ushered me in and offered to bring me food and wine, but I asked to be taken to Nabal first so I could make a proper greeting.

"The master cannot receive you now, Mistress," the steward told me. His eyes darted in the direction of Nabal's bedchamber. "He is, ah, resting."

Was he sleeping off another night of drinking and gambling, or was he exhausted from his incessant bathing? Was it all that he did? "Wake him, then, for I have need of him."

The steward turned red. "He is not asleep, Mistress."

I recalled the two Edomites. "Then please ask him to put aside his women and come to me." Before the steward could protest again, I walked off to the kitchens.

Only the younger female servant was working, stirring a great pot of vegetable porridge in a desultory fashion. When she caught sight of me, her eyes bulged and the spoon fell from her fingers. With a frightened wail, she pulled her head cloth over her eyes.

"Cease that screeching." I went to her and uncovered her face. "You know me, girl. I am the master's wife, Abigail."

"You are a shade, a demon." She cowered in fear. "Do not steal my soul, I beg you."

"I am mistress of this house," I told her firmly, "and I am hungry. Bring food and wine for my husband and me to the great room."

I left her still staring at me and went to the room where my husband received his guests. There were no dogs or remnants of feasting this time, but stains and dirt encrusted the grimy floor. As I waited for Nabal, I thought over what I would say to him about the herdsmen, and how I wanted to help them.

"So, you came back."

I looked up and smiled. "I did."

My husband had washed and dressed, and his linen khiton sported an elaborate hem with much hand embroidery. Gold encircled his neck and wrists,

and on his head he wore the flat, round head covering of an important landowner.

"I sent you to stay in the hills until shearing time," he said as he came to sit in his chair. "You were not told to return."

"I thought I might surprise you."

"You do." He surveyed me. "You look well."

"I am well." I frowned.

Nabal glanced at the floor. "Damned lazy slaves." He shouted for his steward, who came into the room, and pointed at the mess. "When I am finished in here, I want this room scrubbed down. See to it they use boiling water and lye soap."

The steward promised to carry out my husband's wishes and departed. The kitchen servant then came in with food and wine, and I dined with my husband. Nabal did not attempt to make conversation, and I thought he might be in better temper if I let him eat in peace. Worried as I was about Yehud and his family, I could only pick at my meal.

After the servant removed our bowls and cups, I decided it was as good a time as any to tell him my reason for returning. "Husband, I came back to your house because there is trouble in the hill country, trouble that needs your attention."

He leaned forward. "Has something happened to the flocks?"

"The animals are fine and very healthy," I said. "Yehud and his sons take good care of them."

He sat back. "If the animals are well, then what trouble could there be?"

"The herdsmen need food, and they are too busy with the animals to gather what they can from the pasturelands. I need to take back grain, fruit, and cheese for them so they and their families will not go hungry."

His eyebrows rose. "From where do you intend to get this food? It will not come from my stores."

"I thought I might take what extra we have—"

"We?" He laughed. "You own nothing here, wife. You are one of my possessions, that is all."

"I brought a kor of fine wheat and much more to this marriage," I reminded him, exasperated.

"Where it became mine, the day we were wed." He smirked. "You cannot have it back, and you will not give it or any of my stores to the hill people."

"You would have them starve before they can drive the animals to Maon for shearing?" I asked, keeping my tone polite.

"Let them starve." He yawned. "It will save me the year's pay, and I can hire others to take their place." Before I could respond, he rose to his feet. "I have business in town. I suppose you wish to visit your family in Carmel?"

"If I may have the wagon and a driver, yes."

"You need not take the wagon when you can walk." His small eyes glittered with something unpleasant. "Only take care to return before dark. I shall have use for you then."

After my husband left, I sat feeling bewildered and miserably ashamed of my husband. Yehud and his people expected nothing of me, but I could not go

back to the hill country empty-handed. In the kitchen storage pits alone there was enough grain and dried fruit to feed the herdsmen, their families, and the dal. But Nabal would not share his stores, nor allow me to take the food from my zebed.

How could he be so selfish?

I supposed Nabal meant to punish me by making me go on foot to Carmel, but after two days of traveling by wagon, I welcomed the chance to walk. I also needed to think of what to do, although by the time I had crossed the distance between the two towns, I was no closer to finding an answer to my dilemma.

The market had closed for the day, and all the stalls were empty, but I stopped by the old booth where I had sold pots. It had only been a moon since I had been spending my mornings here, and yet it seemed a thousand years ago.

"Abigail?"

I turned to see Rivai hurrying toward me from the town's merchant gate. I grinned and ran into his open arms, embracing him with delight.

"What are you doing here? Where is Nabal?" Rivai held me at arms' length and then pulled me back against his chest. "Adonai, I thought you would not surely return until summer."

"I had to speak with my husband, and see you and our parents." I touched his cheek and admired the sleek, oiled curls of his beard and hair. His eyes were clear and his skin tanned, and he had gained some weight on his lean frame. "You look very well."

"Very well fed, thanks to your friend Cetura. She stuffs us all like fowl to be roasted." He put his arm around me. "Come, I know it will delight our father and mother to see you."

It was strange not walking back to our parents' home, but taking the narrow road to Cetura's house, a big two-level brick house tucked into a cool corner of the town's walls. My feet yearned to change direction and return to the place where I had grown up, so I could again sit among the herbs in the garden and watch the stars come out. Only now I would not long for a husband, for the Adonai had granted me that wish.

Now I would wish that my husband were someone else. Someone with black eyes and gentle hands.

"You must tell us what has happened with you since you left," my brother warned me.

Not everything. "I shall."

Cetura greeted me at the door with a shriek of happiness and a close embrace before she led me inside, where my mother and father were eating their midday meal. My mother recognized me and cried as she said my name and covered my cheeks with soft kisses. My father took me into his shaky embrace and stroked his gnarled hand over my hair.

"My daughter, my daughter," he said, over and over, as if he could not believe his eyes.

"It is me, Father." I rested my cheek against his heart for a moment before I drew back. "Come, sit. I have so much to tell you."

Cetura's sons, Harek and Tul, were also at the

house, in town to deliver their wheat harvest for their mother to sell. They greeted me like a treasured sister while their mother brought tea and little honey cakes. There was some confusion at first as I tried to answer everyone's questions and spoke of my time in the hills.

"It is so beautiful there, Father," I said. "I thought I would miss life in town, but in truth the only things I have missed are you and my friends."

"We hear so many rumors about the people of Paran," Cetura said, "and we have been worried. They say there are bandits in the country who roam about and prey like wolves on the helpless."

I thought of the shepherd and his men. "I have seen no bandits, nor wolves, but there are plenty of sheep and goats." I described Yehud's camp and the women of his family whom I had befriended before adding, "They do not live as we do, but they are a kind and generous people. I think you would like them, Father."

"My grandfather was a shepherd from Paran," he reminded me. "We likely share some distant kinship with them."

We laughed and talked for hours. Rivai told me of his apprenticeship with Amri, and how well his carvings were selling at market now that they were being used as containers for Amri's spice. "No one fears them as pesel as long as they serve a purpose," he said.

Cetura told me about the other merchants of Carmel, and how the coppersmith's son Tzalmon had

scandalized everyone by running off to Hebron with Devash. Happily the families reconciled themselves to the match and had worked out an agreeable exchange of mohar and zebed, so the young couple were expected to return and celebrate their marriage in Carmel.

"It is good that her father is so forgiving," Harek, Cetura's older son, said. "I would have chased down the rogue and given him the thrashing of his life."

His younger brother laughed. "Then you would have bandaged his wounds and carried him to the wedding feast."

As the sun sank to the west, my mother grew weary, so my father took her to their room to rest. It was then that Rivai went to tend to the goats, leaving me with Cetura and her sons. The widow sent the men to deliver some barley to the beer maker, and then we were alone.

"More brought you here than a desire to see us," Cetura said as she sat down beside me. "Now that we are alone, tell me what you would not say before your family."

"You *are* my family," I told her, but she only waited with a knowing look in her eyes. I sighed. "I need food for the people in the hills. I fear they do not have enough to last them until shearing time." I explained how desperate the situation was growing for Yehud and his family.

"Life in Paran is always a struggle," Cetura said sadly. "What can be done?"

"Nothing. I asked Nabal, but he refused. He forbid me touch his stores or my zebed, and said Yehud and his family could starve." I pushed aside my anger over that. "I cannot return to Paran with nothing for them, Cetura. They are in great need, and I especially fear for the children."

"What of the pay your husband owes them?"

"It will be another moon before they drive the flocks to Maon. He says they must wait until then to receive their payment. Then it will take some days for them to sell the animals they receive from Nabal."

"That is a terrible thing," the widow agreed, "but it is not all that disturbs you."

I thought of Keseke's warnings and what the old man at the crossroads had said. It had hovered in the back of my mind all day, but I had refused to face it. "Strange things have happened. Keseke, Nabal's serving woman, gave me food on my journey out to the hill country. I did not like the taste of it, and when she was not looking I fed it to an innkeeper's dog. Yesterday I learned that the dog died in the night after I fed him."

Cetura paled. "Abigail, there can be no mistake?"

"It might have been old cheese, but . . ." No, I could not make that excuse. Old cheese might have made the dog sick, if he had eaten a great quantity of it, but so little? "I think she meant to poison me, even kill me."

"Did she do anything else to you? Did any of her food make you ill?"

I shook my head. "The only other oddity was when I woke the first night in the hill house. I saw Keseke standing over me with a heavy branch. The branch came from the roof, part of which had fallen in."

"Clever, this witch is," Cetura said, anger making her face tight. "She might have beaten you to death in your sleep and then made it look as if the roof had come down on you."

I frowned. "I cannot make sense of it. If she wished me dead, why not try again? Since that first night she has done nothing to harm me." I covered my eyes with my hands. "Perhaps I imagine it all."

"Who sent this woman with you? Nabal?" At my nod, Cetura thumped her hands down on the table. "Then he means you ill."

"Why?" I was confused. "There was no ire between us. He was happy to see me go in his place."

"Think on it, Abigail," the widow urged. "You brought zebed, to his house and were sent away the next day. If you had died in the hill country, he could be rid of you, keep the zebed, and perhaps even find a way to reinstate the debt Rivai owed to him."

I did not think my husband could be capable of such evil intentions, but then Keseke's words came back to me. *Some think he killed his family, so that he would have everything to himself.* "What can I do, Cetura? He expects me to return by sunset."

"You will not go back to Maon tonight," she declared. "It is not safe for you there."

"I cannot hide here. By law he can come and take

me away, and I fear what he might do to my parents and Rivai if I drive him to anger."

The widow slapped her palms together. "That is it. You will go back to the hill country and stay there until shearing time. When you return with the herdsmen and the flocks, you will petition for divorce."

I rubbed my forehead. "Yehud and his family cannot bear another mouth to feed. I cannot even go back to the hill country unless his men take me."

"You must take sanctuary with those people. If only you could . . ." A gleam came into her eyes. "Nabal told you that you could not take food from his stores or your zebed for the herdsmen, were those his words?"

I nodded. "He was very specific about it."

"Not specific enough, child." Cetura looked up as her sons returned from their delivery. "Harek, Tul, load your sturdiest wagon with six kor of wheat and three of barley. Send for the fruit seller and the cheese maker; we will need them to deliver our order tonight."

"You have a craving for raisins and goat cheese, Mother?" Harek teased.

"No. We are sending this all to the hill people."

I nearly fell off the bench. "Cetura, what do you say? I cannot pay for so much. I cannot even buy a single sack of barley for them."

"You do not have to pay for them," the widow said, her smile turning grim. "Master Nabal does. He is responsible for you, and in your absence, he must pay your debts. It is the law."

"He will refuse, and then you and the other merchants will have no payment. I cannot risk it."

"You were a merchant but a moon ago, child, and you have forgotten the law? If Nabal does not pay, then his property will be seized and sold to satisfy the debt." Cetura rested her hands on my cheeks. "Cannot you see the balance of it, child? Nabal did precisely this to your brother. If he is to take refuge in the law, then he must abide by it as well."

It sounded wonderful, and my heart pounded wildly. My excitement faded, however, when I remembered how it felt to have a debt I had never asked for dropped on my shoulders. "Cetura, doing this because Nabal did the same thing to Rivai does not make it right."

"In the eyes of far older law, it does," Harek said. " 'For all things inflicted, so shall you inflict.' "

" 'A life for a life,' " his brother chimed in. " 'A debt for a debt.' "

I closed my eyes. "He shall be so angry."

"Yes, so he shall, but by the time he realizes what has been done in his name, you will be in the hill country, where he cannot easily get to you. We merchants will keep him so busy with the matter of the debt that he will have no time to attend to you. When you return, you will come here, to my house. My sons will protect you until we can win a divorce from the shofet." Cetura turned to her sons. "You will take Abigail back to Paran. Watch carefully on your way; Nabal may have a bright moment and send his men after you."

"Let him," Harek said, and cracked his knuckles with a lazy movement. He was one of the largest men in Carmel, and no one who desired his body sound and whole challenged him to a brawl. "We will send them back."

"After we change their parts around to suit us," Tul tacked on.

Cetura smiled at me. "It will be well, Abigail. I promise." She regarded her sons. "Now, you over-size, adorable mules, let us get the wagon loaded with this wheat. Push it to the back, for I want to make sure there is room for plenty of fruit and cheese."

CHAPTER
13

Cetura's sons made the journey back to Paran a happy one for me. They laughed and joked, and told amusing stories of their wives and children. Both enjoyed their farming life and had many questions about the land near the edge of the wilderness and what grew well there.

"Land like that is good only for terrace farming," Harek pronounced. "Too much climbing about for me."

"But there are pretty shepherd girls who jingle when they walk," Tul said, stroking his beard. "I wager they gild their fingernails and smell of jasmine."

"They trim their nails to keep them from catching on the yarn from their distaffs," I said wryly, "and they mostly smell of the leban they love to drink."

"Leban?"

"Curdled milk."

Tul made a face. "I think I shall be happier to stay farming in the valley with my Shahera."

Harek clapped a sympathetic hand on his shoulder. "Your wife would gouge your eyeballs from your head ere she found you trifling with a shepherdess."

"My eyeballs might go," Tul returned, "but your wife would part you from a certain rod."

"I do not think so," Harek said. "She is very fond of that particular rod."

"Oh, but a rod is a rod," I said, keeping a straight face. "Besides, they are cheap and plentiful at market. She might get another for herself."

Tul shouted a laugh. "There you are, Harek—perhaps you should buy another and keep it as a spare!"

Despite our general merriment, I noticed how watchful Harek and his younger brother were. Nothing moved that did not draw their attention, and they did not stop in the valley of the crossroads.

"We will water our mules and have some food at the stream on the other side of the valley," Tul told me. "There should be no surprises there."

We arrived at Yehud's camp while the sun was still up. As when first I came, Leha walked out to greet us. She looked tired and wan but was pleasant to Cetura's sons and happy to see me.

"I have missed you," she said, taking my hands in hers and pressing her cheek to mine. "We worried you would not return."

"I could not stay in town, for there are too many

people, and too much noise. I did bring back something for the children." I went around to the back of
the wagon.

"Abigail, you should not have—oh!" Leha's mouth
rounded as Harek and I pulled the wagon cover off
the sacks of fruit and wheat, and the stacks of cheeses.
"Is this—" She reached out and then snatched her
hand back. "This cannot be for us."

My throat hurt, and I had to swallow before I
could speak clearly. "It is for you. Wheat and barley,
fruit fresh and dried, and thirty wheels of cheese." I
gave her a sorrowful look. "But no curdled milk.
There was none to be had in Carmel."

"Dearest friend." Leha embraced me. "How can
we repay you for this?" she whispered, still worried.

My husband had done this. His cruelty had wiped
the hope of kindness from these people. In that moment, I was very glad I had agreed to Cetura's
scheme. "You may make me all the honey nut cakes
I can eat."

By now children had come to the wagon, their dull
eyes growing large as they saw the food. While
Harek and his brother unloaded the heavy sacks, I
gave raisin clusters to the young ones.

"You will have to help me test this cheese," I told
them as I tried to lift the first wheel from the wagon.
"I think it is too green, and we may have to feed it
to the goats." I chuckled at the many, eager cries
they gave. "Well, perhaps not."

The cheeses were the largest to be had from Carmel's cheese maker, and far too heavy for me to carry

even one. Two of the oldest boys came on each side
of me, and together we carried it into their mothers' tent.

Bethel rose from her place by the cooking pit and
frowned at me. "What bring you here, wife of
Nabal?"

The boys and I placed the heavy cheese before her,
and I bowed my head. "I have brought food from
the house of my husband." Since he was paying for
it, it was considered a gift of his house. "It is to
express our gratitude for the hard work you and
your people have done in caring for our flocks."

"Your husband would not send a single, withered
fig to us that we had not earned," the old woman
said in her harshest voice. "I know this from years
past, when we were hungry and he let us starve."

I looked into her fierce eyes. There was no denial
I could make, nothing that would redeem my husband. There was not even the desire in my heart to
do so. "Then I would ask you to consider this a gift
of my heart, wife of Yehud."

"You were our honored guest," Bethel said, still
unswayed, "but you are not kin. You are the wife of
our master. We serve you. We do not take offerings
or gifts from you. We are not interested in your
heart."

It was like a slap. Was that how she saw me? As
the patronizing wife of her rich master? Did I mean
nothing more to Yehud's family?

I felt terribly embarrassed. Now I saw my time
with the hill people from their eyes. They had only

tolerated me because they feared Nabal. There was no place for me in the house of my husband, and no sanctuary to be had here.

"Where is Keseke?" I asked, holding on to the ragged edge of my composure. "I shall collect her and leave you in peace."

"Your friend stayed with us until her ankle was healed, and ate our food, and complained all the day and night. Then she slipped away in the dark while we were sleeping." Bethel made a sound of disgust. "She knew we did not have enough, and still she took all the food she could carry. Good riddance to her."

"I am sorry she stole from you." I removed my samla and held it out. "Please accept this." Giving it would not replace what Keseke had taken, but it was a symbol of my shame and contrition.

Bethel ignored it. "You should go now before I truly become angry."

One of the older girls came up and tugged on the seam of Bethel's khiton. "Grandmother, please, it is Abigail. She brought cheese for us, and gave us raisins. Please do not be angry at her. She will take the food away, and our tummies ache."

"Send me out of the camp," I said to the old woman, "but I beg you, keep the food. The children need it." I turned and moved toward the tent flap.

"Abigail."

I looked over my shoulder.

"You cannot go." Bethel put an arm around her granddaughter. "This food must be wrapped and

stored away, and the cheese cut up for the children, and I am too tired to do it."

My shoulders sagged. "Your daughters can do so."

"Is this so? I shall not have the wife of Nabal here, but Abigail of Carmel may stay, if she is willing to live here as our kin, and do her part of the work." She hobbled forward and inspected the cheese. "Where are we to put this monstrosity? It is as big as a ram's head. Two rams' heads. Could you not bring something a little smaller?"

Leha gasped. "Aunt!"

I laughed through the tears stinging in my eyes. "I do not know, but I should say that there are twenty-nine more exactly like it still on the wagon."

From that day forward, Yehud's family treated me just as any other woman in camp. As Bethel had pronounced, I was kin now, and so I was praised and scolded and put to work the same as any of her daughters.

No word came from Maon, nor any of my husband's men to drag me back. I expected them every hour of the first week, and kept close watch, but as the days passed I gradually relaxed and thought less and less about Nabal and how he might try to punish me for disobeying him. My fear I could control. Yehud and his sons would protect me until I could arrange for my divorce.

My dreams, however, did as they pleased, and brought another man into my thoughts.

Every night I dreamed of black eyes watching me, of strong, gentle hands sifting through my hair. In my dreams I heard his voice and watched him dance. Sometimes I heard him sing again, and his songs were like a golden shower over my ears. At the end of the dream, when he came to me—and he always did—I reached for him with eager, open arms. Always, always, I awoke just before I touched him. Often I opened my eyes to find my face already wet from weeping.

The shepherd of the blue mantle danced and sang in my dreams, while I cried in my sleep.

"You are very quiet lately, Abigail," Leha said one afternoon as she helped me remove cooled pots from the oven we were using as a kiln. "Are you missing your family in Carmel?"

"Often. I wish my parents were in better health, so that I could bring them here." I brushed a bit of ash from the lid to a soup pot and handed it to her. "You are not married yet, are you?"

Leha shook her head. "Bethel needs tending, and I am in no hurry to fall in love or begin having babies."

Each married woman in camp seemed to treat her husband differently. Yehud's eldest son came directly to the women's tent to fetch his new wife, and sometimes was so eager for her that he carried her off like a raider. Such displays of passion made the other women laugh out loud, but his wife never seemed to take offense. Indeed, she would giggle herself, all the way out of the tent.

Bethel and Yehud spent their time privately, away from curious eyes, but I sensed a deep and abiding affection as well as respect whenever Bethel spoke of him. Because Yehud had more than one wife, he divided his nights among them. Bethel did not seem to resent her husband's devotion to his other wives, and more than once I heard her urge the younger women to anoint their hair or change their khiton so that they would please the rosh's eye.

Malme, heavy with child, did none of these things. She would sulk throughout the day, pining and sighing for her husband as if her heart was breaking. Yet when her husband came for her at night, her mood changed completely. She would frown and ignore him, complaining endlessly about carrying the burden of their unborn child. Even more astonishing, Malme's husband did not grow angry, but acted as if at fault. He would always coax and plead with her, flattering her and plying her with treats and little gifts until she grudgingly went back to his tent with him.

Malme's belly continued to swell, and as the days passed and her child settled low in her womb, her face, hands, and feet became bloated, as well.

"I fear she will not have an easy time of it," Leha told me. "She has not been eating much and cannot walk more than a few paces without losing her breath."

I had been too young to help my mother with her last pregnancies. "Does the yeled still move?"

"Yes, but not as strongly as before." Leha gri-

maced. "It may be nothing. Some babies do not kick as much just before it is time for them to be born."

Little as I knew about childbirth, this still did not sound promising. "Do you have a midwife?"

"No, but Bethel has seen to the birth of nearly everyone here. She will know what to do for Malme." Leha moved the flat stone over the oven opening and dusted off her hands. "Would you like to go and pick some caper berries with me before you go to my aunt? I saw a ripe patch behind the terebinth grove."

Angry shouts drowned out my answer, and we both turned to see a group of the dal dragging two strange men into the center of camp. There they drove two thick wooden stakes into the ground and tied the strangers to them.

Leha's mouth became a flat, white line. "We must bring the little ones into the tents."

I helped Leha and the other women herd the youngest children away from the scene. Malme began to fuss about the noise, but Bethel spoke sharply to her. When one of the strangers shouted something in a strange language, the women's faces grew fearful.

"Thieving Philistines," Bethel said in disgust, and took my arm. "Leha, stay here and keep the children from the flaps. Abigail will come with me."

I did not know what to expect when Bethel and I walked outside. The shouting of the captives vied with the jeers of the dal, and many knives were drawn.

Afraid blood would be spilled, I put my arm

around the older woman's waist. "Perhaps we should go back into the tent and wait for this to be over."

"No," Bethel said. "Were my husband here, he would take charge. In his place, I must."

"Hebrew trash," one of the captives sneered in our language as he struggled against his bonds. "You only caught us because we are two. Were my kin here—"

"They would be tied up beside you, braying like good Philistine jackasses," one of the dal said. The other men laughed until they caught sight of me and Bethel, and fell silent.

The angry Philistine glared at us. "Why do you bring out your women? Are they who you have fight your battles?"

Bethel released my arm and hobbled forward. "I do not know who brought this erwat dabar into camp," she said to one of the dal, "but you can take them directly where you found them."

Being called as unclean as human waste only goaded the Philistine to become more insulting. "It dresses and sounds like a woman, but it speaks like a man. I know, this must be your melekh."

The dal raised his fist to clout the captive over the head, and then a terribly familiar voice called out, "Hold."

The crowd around the Philistines parted and formed two lines, as soldiers would for their commander. The dal bowed their heads with respect as

the shepherd with the blue mantle walked down the corridor they had formed.

I caught my breath as he ignored the captives and came toward us. After giving me a narrow look, he addressed Bethel.

"I regret that my men have brought violence into your camp, wife of Yehud," he said. His black eyes did not possess a trace of kindness or humor now; the blaze of anger made them glitter like live embers.

"*Now* you bring, and *now* you regret," Bethel muttered. "When our men are gone, when there is no one to decide what is to happen to these men."

He stood. "That is for me to do."

Bethel shook her head. "My husband has spoken to you before. This I know. He will not allow killing here."

"Your husband is gone, and what men you have do not guard you as they should." He gestured toward the captives. "These men came into the pasture and killed four of your goats. We found them roasting the meat in the forest. What if they had taken your daughters instead of the animals?"

Bethel grew furious. "You have a clever tongue, Rea, but you have no say here. You may take your captives and leave this land."

"As you say, wife of Yehud." The shepherd gave me another piercing glance before he walked to where the Philistines were bound to the stakes.

"We should rejoin the other women," I suggested.

Bethel refused to leave. "I must answer to my hus-

band for what happens here, so I must stay and watch," she told me. "If you are afraid, you can go and hide under a blanket."

I was afraid—terribly so, after seeing the fury in the shepherd's dark eyes—but I could not leave her alone, or hide from what he was about to do. Like her, I would stand and serve as witness.

The shepherd said something in a low voice, and the captives were seized and dragged by the dal from the center of camp. When the men had passed outside the horoi stones, they halted and formed a wide circle with the shepherd and the two captives in the center.

"Only so far and no farther," the old woman murmured. "I vow his pride will be his end."

Bethel did not move, and I could not leave her. Helplessly I watched the shepherd as he removed his blue mantle, his simla, and all of his weapons except his staff, and handed them to one of the dal. "What will he do?"

"Fight them." She rubbed her eyes with her twisted fingers in a tired manner. "It is the path he walks, and all he knows."

Two knives were thrown in the dirt before the captives, who were also cut free from their bonds. Both of the Philistines immediately snatched up the knives and held them ready for stabbing.

The shepherd spoke again, and I leaned forward, trying to catch the words.

"You killed animals that did not belong to you,"

he told the captives. "You ate meat that belonged in other bellies."

"That was because we could not find you, goat-herd." The taller, younger captive made an obscene-looking gesture with his hand. "Our king will pay much gold to see you turning over his cook fire." He turned to the other Philistine and asked loudly, "Did you know he was this puny?"

Puny? My jaw sagged. The shepherd may have only been a head taller than me, but he could not be considered small or weak, by any means. Then I realized the Philistines were trying to goad the shepherd to anger.

"You can leave this place unharmed and return to that stinking cesspit of sin you call your home," the shepherd continued, appearing unruffled by the slurs made against him. "All you need do is kill me."

Without warning the Philistines lunged at the shepherd, one from each side, knives flashing.

I covered my mouth with my hand to muffle my cry, and then I saw the shepherd move. He stepped out, brought his staff in a whistling arc, and knocked the first, then the second captive, off his feet. The dal shouted their approval and gathered in, closing the circle around the three men.

"I cannot see what they do." Bethel prodded me forward. "Go to the stones. See what is happening."

I hurried to the boundary of the camp and climbed atop one of the horoi. From there I could see beyond the round wall of men surrounding the three fighting.

The Philistines were on their backs, rolling and groaning, but instead of attacking them while they lay on the ground, the shepherd planted his staff and waited, allowing them to rise. This time the captives did not launch themselves at him together, but exchanged signals by hand and made their own circle around the shepherd.

"Jackals," I heard one of the dal say. "Looking for a weakness."

"They will find none," another replied.

The fight seemed as if it might never end. My fingernails dug into my palms as I watched; my heart lodged in the back of my throat. The captives were determined to kill the shepherd, and slashed their blades in the air. The shepherd did not react until they drew close enough for him to strike, and then he moved. With his staff he dealt blow after blow, bloodying the captives' faces and leaving large, painful-looking welts on their limbs.

He fought like a man who had thrashed a thousand opponents, yet I saw him take no joy in the fight. His expression was not that of a man prevailing over a superior enemy. He had no expression at all.

Did he feel nothing, or did he not permit himself to feel?

Whatever he felt, the shepherd wielded his staff so swiftly and viciously that he was able to strike both captives, one after the other. No matter how they dodged or ducked, neither could avoid the blows. Soon the Philistines, unable to stand straight, were staggering and dripping blood from a dozen wounds.

I nearly fell off the stone when without warning one of the captives whirled and broke out of the circle of the dal, running away and leaving his companion alone with the shepherd. None of the dal tried to pursue him, and I shifted my gaze in time to see the shepherd avoid a knife in his chest and deal a deadly blow to the neck of the captive left behind.

It had been a ruse, to distract the shepherd, and now a man lay dead.

I had never seen a killing before, and even with my distance from the sight, my stomach wanted to empty itself. I scrambled down from the stone and bent over, closing my eyes and taking deep breaths.

"Give me a sword."

It was as if the shepherd had commanded me, and I opened my eyes and straightened in time to see the circle of dal part and the shepherd run out toward the trees. The escaping captive was almost to the forest now; a few more feet and he would be lost from sight.

The shepherd ran so quickly that he crossed half the distance between them before the captive left the clearing. With a fluid motion, the shepherd lifted the long, gleaming sword and threw it. It landed in the back of the escaping captive, who gurgled out a cry and fell over into the grass.

The shepherd slowed to a walk and went to the fallen man. With the efficiency of a herdsman, he took the sword from the captive's back and used it to slit the dying man's throat.

This was the same man who had danced in the rain.

What I felt at that moment made me back away, stumbling over my feet, and then I turned and ran into the camp. Bethel stood waiting where I had left her, and from the paleness of her face I knew she had seen the last man die as I had.

"It is done," she said, the words a bitter rasp. "Come, Abigail. I must send word of this to Yehud. He will make this rabble leave our land before they begin killing us."

"Their leader is the man with the blue mantle, is he not?" When she nodded, my heart constricted. "Who is he?"

The old woman gave me a withering look. "He is David, Abigail."

"David." Surely not—

"Yes, David, son of Jesse, anointed by Samuel, slayer of Goliath. Now David the outlaw, the despised of the king, the hunted."

Leha came out of the tent and hurried over to us. "Malme has passed water and blood, and her pains have started. The babe is coming."

CHAPTER
14

The confrontation with David and the dal left Bethel exhausted, so I agreed to stay and help Leha with the birth. One of the younger women herded the children from the tent, but most of the married women stayed.

Birth was a dangerous time, one the women of the family shared together to the end.

Leha and I propped Malme between us and carried her to the moon tent, where women stayed segregated during the time of their monthly bleeding or when babies were born. Men were not permitted to step foot inside the moon tent, so Malme's husband would not be able to see her when he returned from the herd lands with Yehud.

It was perhaps a good thing that Malme's husband was away, for the young woman screeched vile curses upon his head with every wave of pain. At last, weary of the noise, Bethel told me to fetch a

piece of leather and instructed Malme to bite down on it when the pain came on.

"No more curses," Bethel said, "or the Adonai might mishear you and heap them on the head of your son."

"It hurts, it hurts," Malme moaned.

"Silence," the old woman snapped. "Do not shame the women of this family. You bring a child into the world. It is *supposed* to be painful."

Leha exchanged a look with me before she rose and took Bethel's arm. "You should rest now, Aunt. We will call for you should you be needed." She led her over to a comfortable mat and helped her settle.

I dampened a cloth and wiped the tears from Malme's cheeks. "The little one will be here soon," I told her. "Do you wish for a son or a daughter?"

"I wish this baby never to come," she said, her voice tight. "For it will kill me, and then that old witch will raise it to hate me for dying."

"Then you must live, if only to tell it your side of the story," I said, gently blotting the sweat from her brow. I was trying desperately to remember what Cetura had said about this business of birthing babies. All she had mentioned was that the pains were terrible and that losing too much blood after was what killed the mothers. *Please, Adonai, enough have died on this day.* "Have you and your husband decided on names?"

"He wishes Ephron for a boy," Malme panted out as the next pain gripped her, "and Luz for a girl. They are ugly names. I hate them. I hate *him*."

"Then you must forgive your husband for being a man and persuade him to give your babe a name that sounds joyful to your ears," I told her as I arranged the blanket over her trembling limbs.

The pains were not steady and seemed to subside after a time. Leha joined me and soothed Malme until the young woman drifted in and out of an uneasy sleep.

"I wish we were not so far from a village or town," Leha said quietly. "Pains that come and go as this mean the birth will take at least a night and a day, and she is already so weak."

Part of her weakness was due to lack of food, something everyone in the camp had suffered. But Malme had been eating not to feed only herself, but her child as well. *Yet another life my husband has damaged.*

We watched over Malme and kept her dry and clean. As the sun began to set, two of the other women came to take a turn so that Leha and I could eat and fetch fresh water. We talked as we shared a half loaf of barley and a bowl of bean porridge, and Leha asked what I had seen happen with the dal and their captives.

I told her all, leaving out only the most ghastly details of how David had killed the two Philistines. She paled as she listened, but she did not seem as shocked as I had been by the dal's brutal treatment of their captives.

"They mean to protect us," she said when I had finished. "I know their ways are hard and rough, but

my uncle and cousins would have done the same." Her mouth twisted. "Almost the same. They would have taken the thieves out of sight, so that none of us would see the killing."

"Leha, why did David and his men come here? Why do they stay?" I saw her stiffen. "Your aunt will not tell me, and everyone avoids mention of them. You know the stories of David; to think he is here . . ." I still could not quite believe it. David truly was a legend, the chosen of the Adonai. He may have once been a shepherd, but he was now the future king of our people.

Or was he what Bethel claimed, an outlaw?

Leha avoided my gaze. "My aunt would not be pleased to hear us discussing David. Bethel says it is not a matter for women."

"But this land belongs to my husband," I made the excuse. "If there are killings and strife here, he must be told. He must do something about it."

"Very well." Leha looked from side to side. "Some say David is an outlaw, and his men are slaves, run away from their masters. Just as David runs from King Saul." She made a quick gesture. "I do not think that, for David has always been a lawful man. Besides, they are too many. Would not four hundred slaves be hunted by their masters?"

I had to agree with her—no one would allow so many slaves the freedom to wander or form an army. It would incite other slaves to do the same. Was that what David had done, to make up this army? "Why does the king hunt him? Did he violate the law?"

"No one knows, but there are whispers about the king. They say the spirit of the Adonai has abandoned him from the time Samuel died. That his moods are frightening and change as the weather does. Yehud's cousin Avril has been to court and seen the king with David." She lowered her voice. "Avril says King Saul sometimes acted as if possessed by demons. In his darkest moods, the king would not be soothed by anything but David's songs. Until he picked up and threw a spear at David one day, trying to kill him."

I thought of what David had said at the spring. "Is the king truly hunting them now?"

Leha nodded. "It is why my uncle forbade us to have anything to do with David and the dal. He is a dangerous man, Abigail. King Saul commanded him to slay a hundred Philistines, to prove his loyalty. It is known throughout Judah that David slew *two* hundred and sent their heads to the king."

Small wonder he slit the throat of the Philistine with such ease—he had much practice at killing. *But he took no joy in it, and it was not an even fight,* my heart argued. *There were two of them, armed with knives, while he had but a staff.*

"But if David is so loyal, why does King Saul yet hunt him and his men?" Even for a king obsessed with dark moods, it seemed unreasonable. "What does he think they will do?"

"We cannot know his thoughts." Leha sighed. "But I think it is as Bethel and Malme are. Malme is not so bad as my aunt makes out, you know. A bit

spoiled, but her heart is good. When Bethel looks at her, she sees Malme is young and beautiful and soon to be a new mother, and it tears at her heart."

Because Bethel would never again be any of those things. "Jealousy."

"Leha?" Bethel called.

The younger woman grimaced as she picked up the empty water jug. "I shall have to go to the spring later, I suppose. She will not wish me to leave now."

I looked at the flap of the moon tent. I could stay in here and never face David, or I could help my friend and take the chance of seeing him.

A strangeness twisted in my heart, and I held out my hands. "Let me fetch it."

The bodies of the two slain men had been removed, and the dal resumed their patrol as if nothing had happened. Indeed, there was no sign of what had occurred except for some scuff marks in the dirt at the center of camp. Perhaps David had instructed his men to remove all traces of the incident.

They could not do the same for the images I carried in my mind.

I did not speak to anyone as I left the camp, and I ignored the eyes that watched me go to the spring. No one came to stop me. Why should they? I was only a woman. A fearful, powerless woman who lived among strangers and had no means to protect herself, not even the presence of a caring husband.

I came through the gap and saw David sitting be-

side the water's edge, his arms resting on his knees, his hands linked. He was staring at his reflection on the surface of the water.

I was not startled. Some part of me had known he would be waiting. My skin, perhaps. It had prickled all over with knowledge of him as soon as I entered the gap.

David stood. "Abigail."

"I am only here for water." I could not look into his eyes. I walked to the edge of the spring.

"You were watching me again."

I caught my lip with my teeth and gave a single nod.

"I am sorry for that. Death is not for the eyes of women."

"Women see death every day." I thought of poor Malme, and the struggle she faced to birth her child. Would I have to watch her die, too? "We do not kill people, but we are the ones who must wash and wrap the bodies of the dead." A harsh note entered my voice. "Will we have to do that for the men you slew?"

"We shall burn the bodies," he said softly. "It is the custom of their people."

Did he wish me to praise him for sparing us the funerary duty?

I bent to draw the water Leha needed. I felt awkward and uncomfortable, crouched as I was, for it was as if I made obeisance to him. I went still as David came down beside me.

"Abigail, will you never look upon me again?" He took the jug from my hands before I could fill it and set it aside.

"I dare not." For my faithless heart wanted to do nothing more. "You are the melekh." I said it as much to him as to myself.

A humble potter's daughter had no business speaking to an anointed king.

"I am the same man I was when you saw me dance in the rain."

I closed my eyes briefly. "That man was a shepherd who sang praise to the Adonai." I looked at him. "You are David, slayer of giants and Philistines. A king to be."

"They are all the same man." A shadow of grief passed over his face. "And an outlaw as well."

"I know." When he reached out to me, I stood and stepped away. "Please, I do not know what to do, or to say. I have never seen a man slain. I have no knowledge of kings."

"I am a shepherd, Abigail." His hand fell to his side. "Now I must lead men, and protect Israel, but it is not so different. What the Adonai asks of me will not change who and what I am."

I thought of the terrible blankness in his face as he fought the Philistines. "I was so afraid today," I whispered.

"I know. I would you not have seen it. But know I am not a monster—"

"No." My fingertips rested against his lips. I looked all over his face, memorizing every line, every

color of him. "I was afraid for you. That I would see you slain by those men, with nothing I could do to save you. How could you be so reckless? To give them knives, to fight them both at once?" My voice grew choked. "Don't you understand? I was not afraid of you, but *for* you. The Adonai forgive me, but I was *glad* when you killed them."

My own words shamed me to my bones, and I burst into tears.

"Shhh." His arms came up around me, and he held me tenderly.

When I could control my emotions, I pulled back and dashed the tears from my face. "I must go," I said, blindly reaching for the jug.

"Wait." His palm cradled my damp cheek as he made me look at him. "In this moment, I could compose a thousand songs about the beauty of your eyes."

"They are not beautiful." I sniffed. "They are red and swollen."

"So they are, and still they haunt my dreams."

He dreamed of me. No, no, he could not. Kings did not dream of common maidens.

"I came to tell you that my men and I must leave here when the sheep are driven to Maon for shearing." His thumb traced my bottom lip. "Abigail, when we go, will you come with me?"

Go with him? The heat ebbed from my limbs as quickly as he had awoken it with his touch. By asking me to go with him, David was inviting me to be his lover, perhaps even his wife.

Yet I was already married.

Everyone knew the law over the respectability of women. A man might take more than one wife, but a woman could not have more than one husband. A married woman could not take any man other than her husband as her lover.

Any woman who did not follow the law was an adulteress, and as such sacrificed all she had brought to the marriage to her husband, as well as what she had gained from him.

Such as a debt she had married him to pay, or a debt he had been forced to pay for her.

"I cannot." I moved away. "You know nothing of me."

His mouth curved. "I know that you are my little dove of peace. I would spend a thousand nights in your gentle arms."

This had to end. "We will never spend a single night together. David, I am not free. I belong to another man. I am married."

"What?"

I met his bewildered gaze. "I am Abigail of Carmel, wife of Nabal. My husband owns the flocks you have been guarding, and this land you and your men patrol. He is master of these people, and me."

David said nothing for a long time. He stared down at me, and anger made his eyes into black fire.

At last he asked, his voice strained, "Why did you not say before?"

"Before." I stared at him. "You speak of the time when we first met here, and you did not tell me who you were?"

The side of his mouth made a bitter curl. "I was wrong. You have the eyes of a dove and the heart of a lioness."

"I am neither bird nor beast. I am the wife of another man, and you are an outlaw king. We must never see each other again." I drew the water Leha needed and tucked the jug against my hip. "Farewell, Melekh David."

He did not stop me. He seized me. Water from the jug splashed over the rim and splashed down the front of my khiton. He moved as lightning struck, and that as much as the cold wetness startled a cry from me.

David took the jug from my hands.

"Please, Melekh, I—" I gasped as he tipped the jug and poured the rest of the water down the front of me. "What have you done?"

"No more than you have done to me. I want you to know this fire you have built inside me, Abigail." He tugged me against the front of his body and held me fast. "It burns without cease." He pressed my hand under his, so that my fingers were spread over the beating of his heart. "Can you feel the heat of it?"

I felt wet and frightened. "I have done nothing to you. Please, release me."

"But you have." He dropped to his knees and rubbed his cheeks and nose against the wet cloth clinging to my belly. "The sight of you captures my eyes. You distract me from my purpose. You make me yearn for nothing but you."

My hands came up on their own accord and touched his head. "David." His name could be the only thing

I said for the rest of my life and I would be content. "David, you must not do this. I am married to another man." And in that moment, I hated Nabal with every part of my being. "Even were I not, I am but the daughter of a poor man. I have no family and no royal blood, no nahalah. I can give you nothing."

"I know what you did for Yehud and his family. How you brought food for them so they would not suffer. You would save them and let me go hungry." He looked up at me. "I starve for you, Abigail. For the love of the Adonai, feed me."

I should have pushed him aside. Even if he was a king to be, he had no right to touch me like this. But his hands were on my hips, and his hair in my hands, and I could not breathe anymore for wanting him.

"Yes." Slowly he rose, making a path up the wet cloth of my khiton with his mouth. His face and chest were wet as he straightened, and the sun glinted on the droplets beading his thick dark lashes.

Was he weeping for me? If he was, it would tear my heart in two. "I beg you leave me go."

"I can kill giants and cross mountains, little dove, but I cannot stop touching you." His hands moved over me, caressing my shoulders, pressing the soaked fabric over my breasts. "I know we cannot be together. I know." He looked down at my body, outlined as it was by my wet khiton. "But if I am to burn, I would you give me one last sip from your fountain. If I am to die of hunger, let me taste you before I wither away to bone."

He was not withering. Desire made his male part

thick and hard where he pressed it against the curve of my belly. The words spilling from his lips were beautiful and thrilling, like those of his songs, but I understood what he was asking. He desired me. He wanted to put himself inside me. He wanted to lie with me and give me his child.

Desire was a terrible thing. I knew, for I had burned and starved for him. As I did now.

His rough hands eased my khiton from my shoulders. To my shame, I remembered that I wore no shift under it. The wet wool clung, and he could not slip it down any farther than my breasts.

"Help me," he murmured against my brow. "I must see you. I must."

I shook my head, but my back touched stone, and he lifted me off my feet and stepped between my legs, so that I straddled him.

"You cannot deny me."

I did not wish to. I wanted him. I wanted to be naked with him. As if we were in one of my dreams, my hands lifted again, and I bared my breasts to his gaze. "No," I said, my voice breaking, "I shall not deny you."

David gave me more beautiful words, poetry murmured upon my skin as he nuzzled and kissed my breasts. His touch spread the fire through my body. Our lower halves were so tightly pressed together that they wrung the water from my khiton to drip in steady streams. I heard as if from a distance the pattering of the water and the rasp of his beard as he suckled me.

What an eager child passion was, to nurse so strongly.

The stone at my back became prickly grass, and David's arms my bed. The weight of him atop me was heavy, almost to where I could not draw a breath, but then he shifted. His mouth traced my brows, the length of my nose, my lips. I clung to him, dizzy and bewildered by the heaviness of my limbs and the deep, hollow ache between my legs.

Someone said something, and David lifted his head to look around. I went still.

"Abigail?" It was one of the children from camp, Yehud's youngest son, a boy of five. "Are you hurt? Why does Melekh David hold you down so?"

David rolled over and stood, helping me to my feet and hiding me behind him so I could straighten my garments. He gazed down at the boy. "Men do not hurt women. We protect them."

Yehud's son gave him a solemn nod.

He placed a hand on the boy's shoulder. "Abigail needs a man to protect her as she walks back to camp. Will you do this for me?"

"I shall, Melekh David." The boy threw his shoulders back and imitated his father's stern glare. "No one will harm Abigail while I am with her."

"Good." David came to me and before I could speak and brushed his mouth over mine. "Look after her well, boy. She is a good wife."

CHAPTER
15

Malme's labor continued through the night and into the next morning. Leha and I spelled each other, but I could not snatch more than a few moments of sleep. I felt my mouth still damp with his kiss, my body still warm from his touch, and my heart became like a stone in my breast.

If this was what it meant to find a dream, then I did not wish to dream, ever again.

As dawn came, the young mother's battle to bring forth her child turned worrisome. Bloody fluid trickled from between her legs, and her skin turned cold and clammy. The pains that had caused her to moan and complain now wracked her body with agony.

Leha drew me aside. "I cannot feel the baby's head. I think it may be turned the wrong way." She glanced over at Bethel, who had not risen from her mat. "My aunt is not well enough to attend her, and none of the other women know what to do."

"Can we send for a midwife?"

She shook her head. "The journey takes a day, and by the time she comes I fear it will be too late to save them."

"Why are you two standing here gossiping?"

We both turned toward the familiar, complaining voice, and watched as a bedraggled Keseke hobbled over to us, supporting her weight with a stick stripped of bark.

She looked from Leha to me. "What do you here? There is a baby to be born. Tell me what you have done, and how she does."

Leha hesitated, and then told Keseke everything that had happened through the night. "Have you ever seen such a birth?"

"I had two of my own try to come out that way." She noticed my stare. "I was not always a servant. My children died with my husband, of the spotted sickness."

I wanted to touch her arm and tell her how sorry I was, but I was still too angry with her. "How fortunate that you decided to come back."

"You may take up your stick and beat me later, Mistress," she advised me. "For now, I shall go to Malme and see what can be done."

I insisted she wash first, which she did without complaint, and I watched her carefully. If she tried to hurt anyone, I would be the one to stop her.

Malme's entire body dripped with sweat, but she could no longer be roused from her stupor. Keseke eased down beside her and used her hands to check the position of the child.

"It is as you said," she told Leha. "The baby's feet have already emerged. It is lucky that I have small hands. You will have to hold her down for me. This will hurt her and make her cry out."

Leha and I took position on either side of Malme, while Keseke knelt and pushed her hand into the young woman's body. Malme reacted with a terrible scream and writhed under our hold.

"Keep her still!" Keseke snapped.

I held on and prayed.

It seemed to take forever, and Malme screamed several times. Then her entire body went rigid, and Keseke eased her hand back.

"Now push," she told Malme. "Push!"

Malme's exhausted face turned bright red. A gush of blood and fluid came, and then I saw a round head. Malme screamed one final time, and the baby seemed to pop out of her body like the clay seal from a bottle of fermenting wine.

"Here now," Keseke said, holding the squirming little baby over his mother's belly, "you have a fine son."

A firstborn son was something to celebrate, and the men preceded to do just that. The younger wives joined them, but the older women, Leha, and I stayed with Malme and her baby. The new mother stopped bleeding as soon as the baby was put to her breast, and she drifted into a healing sleep, still cradling her new son.

"He is a greedy one," Leha said, gently turning

the baby to suckle at his sleeping mother's other breast. "Big and healthy, too. It is almost as if he grew fat while his mother grew thin."

I laid a hand on the top of his round head. He had a dark pink, wrinkled face and tiny black curls. His hair felt softer than lamb's wool. "There is no creation of the Adonai's more precious or amazing than a newborn child."

"We have your friend to thank for that," Leha said, nodding toward Keseke, who was crouched over a water basin and cleaning Malme's blood from her hands.

My smile faded. "Yes."

I went over to join Keseke. I had no desire to speak to her, but there were matters to be settled. Such as, "Why did you come back?"

"Why not? There was nowhere for me to go. I could not walk all the way back to Maon, and there are no caves near here. Trees do not make comfortable beds." She nodded in the direction of the forest.

"Yet you left before," I pointed out. "You remember, when you stole the food from the people who cared for you."

"There are things out there that are much worse than here, Mistress. I did not know this when I fled." She shrugged. "Now I do."

Had she no conscience? "Keseke, you *stole* from these people. You knew they had little food left, and that their children were hungry, and yet you did this. How could you?"

"I was afraid." She glared at me. "No one here

adopted me as their daughter, did they? No, I was only tolerated because of you."

I started to argue with her and then remembered how I had felt when Bethel had heaped her scorn upon my head. "What you did was wrong."

Her scowl deepened. "I saved the life of Malme and her child, did I not? Does that make up for my theft?"

"A good deed in exchange for a bad one; that is your thinking?" She nodded. "Then how will you make up for trying to take my life?"

She went silent and stared at her hands, and then rubbed them against her khiton. At last she met my gaze. "How did you know?"

"It matters not, only that you tried twice to kill me," I told her. "What do you plan to exchange to make up for them? Must I wait until you can deliver my first two children?"

She rested her face against her hand and wrapped an arm around her knees. Curled over as she was, she began to rock back and forth. "He will never give you children. He did not want you for his wife. He wanted your dowry. Nothing pleases him unless he can have it to himself."

Cetura had suspected as much, but I had been hoping the evil had come from another source. Still, I had to be sure. "Did my husband order you to kill me?"

Keseke became angry. "I warned you, did I not? But you would not listen."

I pretended to think. "I recall no words of warning when you gave me that poisoned bread and cheese

on the journey here. Nor before that night, when you made to beat my head in while I slept."

Shame and defeat dulled her eyes. "I could do nothing else. The master told me that it was your life, or mine. I did not wish to die."

"Yet you failed twice to kill me," I pointed out. "Why did you not try again? There were many times you might have succeeded. I ate all the food you prepared; I slept like a child in your presence. There was nothing to stop you."

"Nothing? What of you, calling me friend instead of servant?" She flung out one hand. "Bringing me here with you, sharing your food and fire, other kindnesses too many to number. You set out to defeat me. You bored into my heart like a worm of goodness."

Had the woman a single drop of shame in her body? "Yes, I can see how horrible it must have been for you."

"It was." She thumped her breast. "I could not do as I had been told. It was the goodness in you, it blinded me." She ducked her head. "It made me hope when I had vowed never to feel so again."

"Oh, Keseke." I wanted to throttle her and embrace her at the same time. "If you did feel that way, then what were you to tell Nabal? How would you explain your failure?"

"I did not intend to die for you, if that is what you mean," she snapped. "I thought when the time came to return to Maon that we would flee him to-

gether. Only I could not think of how to tell you what he had done, and what I had tried to do."

"I could see where you might have trouble finding the right words." I made my voice an imitation of her crossest tone. " 'Oh, Mistress, let us run away together into the wilderness so that I do not have to try to poison you again or crush your skull in the night.' "

"Exactly so." Her mouth softened. "I do not think anything bad will ever happen to you. It is as if the Adonai protects you with a shield no one can see." She gave me an uncertain look. "Do you forgive, Mistress?"

"You will call me Mistress no more," I said. "To you I am Abigail."

"Abigail." Keseke said it carefully.

"You will work hard for Yehud's wives and make up for that which you stole from them," I continued sternly. "And you will never follow any orders. I am making you a free woman, of free will. Whether you choose to stay here or leave, you are responsible for your actions from this moment hence."

"You cannot free me," she muttered. "The debt of my husband to yours is too large; my servitude is for life."

"I am still the wife of Nabal. I may incur debt, or I may release it. That is the law. I release you from your debt to my husband." I kissed her brow. "There, it is done. You serve no one but yourself."

"Foolish girl, to set free a servant so. I can see you

will need careful guidance if you are not to beggar yourself after this divorce." Keseke sighed. "I shall stay with you then"— she eyed me—"as friend and companion."

I smiled at her. "As you have always been."

The food I had brought to Yehud and his family gave them time to gather and replenish their stores. By the time the sheep were ready to be driven to Maon for shearing, the hill people had regained their health and were once more strong and vigorous.

The same could not be said of the dal. Four hundred men required a great deal of food, and the southern shepherds had exhausted the local supply of game. Hunger made the men grow gaunt, yet no complaints were made, and the patrols around the camp and the herds never ceased.

"I would feed them all," Leha said one day, watching the patrol, "but they are too many. We cannot share without depriving our own children again."

I knew how she felt. That morning I had seen two of David's men sharing a root from a broom tree. Only the worst kind of hunger would drive someone to subsist on such bitter stuff. "They were to leave after the flocks are driven to Maon for shearing."

"They must go before that, or soon they will not have the energy to make such a march," Leha predicted.

The dal were scrupulous in their dealings with Yehud's family, even at cost to themselves. When a young goat somehow escaped the sheepfold during

the night and was found by the patrol, the dal might have taken the kid to their camp, roasted, and devoured it without anyone the wiser. Instead, they brought the animal back to the camp, where they presented it to Yehud, along with a warning about the shepherds to the south, who had been raiding towns and villages for food.

"They cannot exist much longer on roots and grass," Bethel said to me one evening as we were readying the children for sleep. She tugged a nightdress over the head of one small child and kissed her granddaughter before tucking her under a soft warm blanket.

I thought of David eating weeds to stay alive, and the good meal in my belly turned to a solid lump. "What can be done for them?"

"I have spoken to my husband, but it is as Leha says. We cannot share with them and have enough for our own kin."

I thought of the raids to which the southern shepherds had resorted. "Melekh David will not lead them against anyone to obtain the food they need, will he?"

Bethel shook her head. "David has prevented too many such attacks to indulge in one himself, no matter how hungry his men are. He has his most trusted men on patrol, and leads the others in long hunts every day. My husband said of late they are killing and eating wolves and lions."

I grimaced. The flesh of predators could not be much better than bitter roots. Part of me was glad to

know this, though, for it explained why I had not seen David of late. Instantly I felt foolish for even thinking such a thing. "We must pray for them."

"Pray they leave these lands and find new graze before they begin burying each other," Bethel said.

Keseke overheard my conversation with Bethel and came to me. "There is an old farm in the hills, beyond the forest of the spring. It is abandoned, but there is wheat growing wild and many fig and olive trees." She took a twig and drew a crude map of the farm in the dirt.

I examined her drawing. "How do you know this?"

"It is where I stayed when I went wandering." That was how she referred to her theft and flight during my absence. "There is not enough food for half of four hundred, but what could be gleaned from the fields will be better than lion meat."

I regarded her carefully. "You did not have to return here, then. You might have stayed at that farm and lived well."

"I have no talent for farming, and the house was atrocious. Swine would be uncomfortable in such a place." She sniffed and went to grind grain for the morning bread.

I smothered a chuckle. It would seem that Keseke, who claimed she had no heart, was yet the owner of a very guilty conscience.

Once the children were all on their mats, and the last of the daily chores completed, I slipped out of the tent and went to walk along the perimeter of the

camp. As no one had come from Maon for me, I no longer felt afraid of being alone, even in the darkness.

I meant only to speak to one of the dal about the abandoned farm, but as soon as I called to the patrol, a familiar figure came out of the shadows.

"Melekh David." I bowed my head with deliberate, deep respect. Such respect would have to remain like a wall between us until the time I returned to my family. "I have learned of something that may be helpful to you."

His mouth formed a bitter curve. "Is it the arrival of forty wagonloads of grain, sent from the king's silos, along with a royal pardon for imaginary crimes?"

"No, but should such come along, you will be the first to hear of it. Unless I encounter another army of men in need of food and forgiveness."

My serious response made him utter a short laugh. "Oh, my dove, you always bring gladness to my heart."

While he was in this better mood, I related what Keseke had told me and pointed in the general direction of the farm. "She says it may not be enough, but I thought you might use what was there for your journey."

The good humor left his eyes. "We cannot leave until the flocks are driven to Maon."

I grew angry. "David, we are all aware that your men are starving. Are you?"

"I suffer with them every day, little dove. The Adonai shall keep us safe and whole."

"The Adonai does not have to march on patrol each day," I said. "You know that you and your men cannot stay here. Yehud and his sons will look after my husband's flocks. Go, before the shadow of death steals into the valleys and your men begin dying."

"What of you?" He glided the side of his thumb over my cheek. "Who will look after you, care for you, little dove? Who will warm your sleeping mat at night, and wake you to joy in the morning? Not this husband who abandons you like this."

If he thought me unhappy, he might never leave me alone. Better he think me a content wife, eager to return to her husband. "No one. I choose to be here, in my husband's place. In all things, I do my husband's will." I took a step back. "Do not ask me to say more, Melekh David. I must go. Peace be upon you." My khiton flared out as I showed him my back.

Hands caught my shoulders and held me in place. "Do not fly away yet," he murmured. He pulled away my head cloth and buried his face in my hair. "When the flocks go, so shall you, back to your husband. Is it not so?"

"I must."

"I would keep my promise to you, Abigail." David tucked my head cloth in my hand and closed my fingers over it. "Will you come to the spring tomorrow at dawn?"

I could barely force the words out. "I cannot. I *dare* not."

"I give you my word; all I shall offer you is that which I promised." He hesitated, digging his fingers

into my shoulders. "Let me do this, little dove. Let me have this moment with you, and that will be all I ask of you."

"Dawn, I shall be there." I felt his fingers slip away, and hurried back into camp.

CHAPTER
16

I did not sleep that night, tormented as I was by my own thoughts. I knew going to the spring was unwise, even foolhardy, considering what had happened between us there. A man might make promises, but desire was like a veil of forgetfulness. I could not let David wrap that around me again.

My life was not a dream.

The accounting was finished, and the disks I would give my husband lay in a sack by my sleeping mat. Yehud had been rigorous about the precise count of adult animals, new lambs, and the winter losses. His counts and mine matched down to the last animal, and I wondered if it would please my husband to know that his flocks had increased by a full one-third over the winter months.

Nothing pleases him unless he can have it to himself.

Nabal had been willing to allow his herdsmen to starve because it would save their pay. He had ordered Keseke to kill me so that he could have my

zebed without the inconvenience of keeping the wife that went with it. He had, I felt sure, swindled my brother into losing the eight maneh of gold—if that was even the true amount. Rivai had been made to drink himself senseless that night; Nabal could have invented any figure that pleased him, and my brother would likely not have known the better of it.

My husband had a great deal for which to answer, and repent. And I knew in my heart that he would not. Such a man did not have a conscience. Even if my petition of divorce was granted, he would find some way to take vengeance on me and my family.

I rose before dawn and dressed in my best khiton. I brushed my hair until it shone, but I did not braid it or bind it to my head. I made my way past the sleeping women to the tent flap and stepped out into the darkness.

I had not gone ten paces before Keseke whispered my name furiously. I sighed but did not turn around. "Go back to sleep. I am going to fetch water."

"In your finest robe, with your hair down? I think not." She came to me and thrust an empty jug into my hands. "Here. At least make it *appear* as if you are going to fetch water."

I curled my hand around the wide belly of the jug. "My thanks."

"Thank me in nine moons, when you are pushing a child from your womb and cursing him for abandoning you," she snapped.

"There will be no child." There would never be. I would not lie with David. No man would have me

after I divorced Nabal. It struck me what that would mean in my life. A divorced woman was only little better than an outcast. Like the gerusa, I would be fortunate if people even spoke to me. *If Nabal does not have me killed.*

Keseke waved me on. "Go. You must return soon, or the others will suspect."

My steps dragged as I walked to the spring and grew slower the nearer I came to it. I did not want this to be the last time I saw David. I did not want to see him now, and love him any more than I did. I bounded from one side of my heart to the other, uncertain and afraid.

The spring was deserted, and so I had a little time to compose myself. I filled the jug, lest I forget to do so later, and set it aside. Then I removed my head cloth and shook out my hair. This once, he would see me as a husband would.

"You are early this morning, little dove."

I turned around in a circle, but saw no one. "Where are you?"

"Look up."

I did, and saw him perched on the top of the tallest of the rocks surrounding the spring. "David, what are you doing up there?"

"Leading us not into temptation." He produced a small lyre, and glided his fingertips across the strings. "I did not sleep last night, for the words that rushed into my head. I cannot dance, not now, but I would sing the song I made of them for you now, Abigail."

I sat down at the edge of the spring.

David plucked a few strings, finding the softest, lightest of notes, and then nodded to himself and strummed his fingers across them. The sound of the lyre was honey to the ears, and made me smile in spite of myself. Watching my eyes, he sang:

Adonai is my shepherd;
I shall not want.
He makes me to lie down in green pastures;
He leads me beside the still waters.
He restores my soul;
He leads me in the paths of righteousness
For His name's sake.
Yea, though I walk through the valley of the shadow
of death,
I shall fear no evil;
For You are with me;
Your rod and Your staff, they comfort me.
You prepare a table before me in the presence of my
enemies;
You anoint my head with oil;
My cup runs over.
Surely goodness and mercy shall follow me
All the days of my life;
And I shall dwell in the house of the Adonai
Forever.

I found myself sitting as one of the children did when Leha told a tale, so rapt was I. As the final golden notes from the lyre slipped away, I sighed my delight.

"Does my song please you as well as the last?" he asked me.

"It is lovely, David. More beautiful than I can say."

"It will be my memory of you, and my comfort when we part." He set aside the lyre, and his face became a mask of grief. "I shall try hard to believe the words, for they surely come from the Adonai. He is my only haven now."

I wished that I had something of his poetry and music, so that I could give him the same in return. All I could offer was a smile, and it was a pitiful one, indeed.

"Will you promise me something?" he asked. "If there is ever a need in you for something only I can give, will you come to me?"

"You are to be king. I would not presume—"

"You have a rich husband, and I may be dead before winter." He made a careless gesture, as if his life meant nothing. "Promise me anyway. Promise that if I am alive, you will find me."

I would never go to him. "I shall."

He nodded and tucked the lyre into his hagor. "We are sending for supplies and expect them to arrive shortly, and then we will journey to Ziklag. I shall think of you often, little dove. Do not forget your vow."

David did not climb down to embrace me, as I had hoped. He bowed to me, as if I were some queen, and then slipped away.

I sat until the sun was full up, softly repeating the

words of his song to myself until they were burned
forever upon my heart.

The time to drive the sheep to Maon came two
days later, and I readied myself for the journey.
Yehud and most of his sons would not only drive
the sheep, but would shear them when they arrived
at my husband's house. That, too, was part of the
service Nabal demanded of the herdsmen, and they
would not be given their portion until that last fleece
was sheared.

"You should remain here," Bethel fussed. "I do
not trust your husband to leave you alone."

"He might yet send men here to retrieve me," I
reminded her.

"If he does, they will have to go through the dal.
They intend to remain here to protect us until Yehud
and the men return."

I was surprised to hear that. After the farewell we
had exchanged at the spring, I thought David and
his men would leave as soon as the flocks had.

"I must settle things with my husband and family," I told her, "but I shall not stay away long." I
hesitated. "Bethel, both my parents are old and ill. If
it seems that Nabal wishes to take revenge on us for
what I have done—"

"Bring them with you," she said firmly. "I would
appreciate the company of a few more people my
age, and they are kin now, as you are. Make no protest, for I know Yehud would say the same."

I embraced her. "My thanks."

Keseke would not allow me to journey back to Carmel by myself.

"My ankle is better, and you will need a witness to aid your petition. I shall tell the shofet all that the master has done." She sighed. "Though it means my imprisonment for harming you, I deserve it."

"I recall no time that you harmed me," I said.

She gave me a suspicious look. "You would lie for me?"

"It is not a lie. You never succeeded." I gave her my surliest look. "It is the only way I shall allow you to come back with me, so you may as well agree now. Or you may stay here and help the women prepare to move the camp when we return."

"Queen of Heaven, do not leave me here." She sent a nasty look to the milk-filled goatskin churn suspended from poles outside the tent. "They intend to make liters of that wretched sour milk for the journey, and who better than an old woman to sit and rock the churn?"

"I would not subject you to such torment." I shooed her along. "Go, pack your things. We leave at dawn."

Driving the herd made the journey twice as long as it took by wagon, but Yehud and his sons insisted we ride their mules while they walked most of the way. Long years of herding made their legs accustomed to the distance, and they seemed to prefer staying close to the flock.

Making camp was enjoyable, and the task of preparing food for the men easy with the stores Bethel had sent along with us. The tents the men had brought were so small they were suitable only for sleeping, and even so, the one Keseke and I shared barely had room for that.

"If you snore, I shall shake your shoulder," I told her as we curled up together.

"If I do not snore, shake my shoulder," she snapped, "for I shall no longer breathe."

We remained together with the men and the sheep as far as the outskirts of Maon, where we parted ways.

"I will tell the master that we left you back in Paran," Yehud said as he bid me farewell.

"Would it be better, perhaps, not to speak of me at all? If Nabal asks, you can say you do not know where I am." That would not be an untruth, for Yehud did not know the location of Cetura's house in Carmel.

He reluctantly agreed. "But when we return to Paran, you will come with us, Abigail. Were I to leave you here, Bethel would beat me without mercy."

I smiled. "I would not see her make you suffer so."

Keseke and I walked the road between towns, and I noticed that the closer we came to Carmel, the more silent she grew.

"I shall explain everything to my family," I assured her. "They will not resent you."

"You have a forgiving family."

The sun drew near its zenith by the time we reached town. The market was just closing, so I was able to greet my friends among the merchants packing up their goods. The warm welcome they gave me was punctuated by demands that I visit their households. Shomer was especially adamant.

"Cetura told us of your seeking divorce from Nabal," he said. "Until the petition is granted, it is best if you not be where your husband can find you."

"Shomer, was he very angry about the debt of food?" I asked.

"He came here himself to argue over the bills he received. The fruit seller had to summon the shamar when he threatened to have his men tear down his stall. He would not pay until the shofet threatened to take his land and house from him." The rug seller sighed. "Truly, Abigail, I had hoped this man would be good to you, but I have never known such a jackass. I prayed to the Adonai you would not forgive him and return to his house."

Keseke listened closely to every word Shomer uttered, but remained silent, casting only a few odd glances at me.

"That will not happen." Dread forced a cold knot in my belly. "I shall come to visit tomorrow, if I may."

"You must. We have a new grandchild to present to you, and my wife wishes to hear all about the hill country." He held his hands up as if beseeching the Adonai. "And you know what she is like when she is denied that which she wants."

We left the market and went on to Cetura's house, where Keseke paused outside the door. "I would go and see a friend of mine, Abigail. We have not met since last winter, and she lives in a house but two streets from here."

She was yet nervous about meeting my family. "My friend, you will not be treated badly here. I shall tell them everything you have done, and they will see you as I do."

"Yes, yes, but I would see my friend first." She gave me a long-suffering look. "You would not deny me this small pleasure, would you?"

She had had so little in her life that I could not. "You will come here directly after," I said. "I do not want you where Nabal or his men might see you."

"They never noticed me before; they will not see me now." As if on impulse, she leaned over and kissed my cheek. "I shall not fail you, Abigail."

"Of course you won't." I smiled at her. "Only remember that you are among friends here."

After Keseke went off to visit her friend, I went into the house. Cetura and my mother greeted me, but my father and Rivai were gone for the afternoon.

"Amri needed help sorting goods he bought from an Egyptian," the widow explained, "and your father wanted the walk."

I knew the midday heat would feel good on my father's painful joints, and Amri would take care that he did not overexert himself. "I brought some figs from the hill country, and the honey cakes they

make." I gave her the sack of fruit and cakes that I carried. "They are almost as good as yours, Mother, except they do not have nuts."

My mother only murmured something vague, and the looks she gave me were quite puzzled. As Cetura and I were picking over some lentils for a stew, Chemda said, "You are very brown, and there are streaks in your hair. You do not look much like my daughter, Abigail."

I was tanned from my weeks working in the sun—most often I had worn one of the sleeveless khitons favored by Leha and her sister—and my head cloth always slipped to my shoulders after a time.

I examined my arms ruefully. "It is still me, Mother. It is but a darker version."

"I think you are much shapelier since last we saw you," Cetura put in. "You have grown into a woman's body."

My waist and thighs seemed smaller since I had gone into the hills, but my breasts had become fuller and larger. I felt slightly embarrassed by their scrutiny and tugged at my khiton. "We have been working hard to prepare the camp to move."

"Where will the hill people go, once this shearing is finished?" the widow asked.

I explained that this would be the last year Yehud watched over Nabal's flocks. "The master of the shepherds in the southland has dismissed his men for drunkenness and stealing from the local farmers. He sent word that he sought to hire new men, and Yehud went to speak with him just before we left.

They struck a good bargain, and so the herdsmen will be tending to his flocks for the winter months."

Cetura nodded her approval. "Your husband will have neither men nor wife to piss on now."

Her slightly crude remark provoked my mother to slap her arm. "Cetura, for shame! You should not speak so in front of the children."

The widow and I regarded the two puppies sleeping at my mother's feet. Harek had brought them as a gift for her just after she and my father moved in with the widow, to help calm her agitation. Cetura claimed Chemda was fascinated with the young dogs and that they seemed to have done much to keep her mind from wandering.

"She still insists they are your and Rivai's siblings now and then," Centura admitted.

"I do not mind," I told her. "If she must sleep with something, let it be a pup instead of a goat."

I helped the widow prepare the evening meal while we waited for the men to return, but a feeling of unease set in as the hours passed and Keseke had not yet returned. I went to the window several times to look out into the street, but saw no sign of her.

"She did not say how long she would visit," I told myself. "She promised not to fail me."

Cetura joined me at the window. "Did she tell you the name of this friend she went to visit?"

"No, only that she lived two streets over from your house."

The widow frowned. "Abigail, there are only tanners on that street, and their wives do not live there

for the smell. All their women dwell on the other side of the town."

I picked up my samla and wrapped it around me. "I shall go and find her."

Cetura forbade me to leave alone. "With things as they are between you and your husband, you cannot simply walk about without someone to watch over you. You must wait for your brother to come home."

A short time later my father returned without Rivai, and greeted me sadly. "We were readying to leave Amri's when the shamar came for Rivai."

Nabal. "Father, did they arrest him?"

"No, they needed him to come to attend to a woman they found outside the merchant's gate. She was left there to die after she had been attacked and beaten. She asked for your brother."

"Keseke." Before anyone could stop me, I ran out of the house and down the road, heading toward the market.

Not halfway there, I saw my brother and Amri walking toward me. In my brother's arms was a huddled form swaddled in blankets.

"Keseke?"

"It is she," Rivai said. "We are taking her to Amri's house; it is closer. No, do not touch her, Abigail. Her bones are broken."

I looked at the blood dripping from the blankets he had wrapped around her. "Which bones?"

Amri pulled me back and made me face him. His eyes were bleak. "All of them, Abigail. She was beaten until they broke all of them."

CHAPTER
17

It seemed to take forever to walk the short distance to Amri's house. I could not think; I could only hover near Rivai and try to see Keseke's face. The blanket covered most of it, only showing her bloodied mouth and broken nose.

My brother carried her in, and Amri put several blankets over his largest worktable. "Place her here, Rivai. Abigail, light the lamps so I may examine her."

My hands shook as I used a burning straw to light the wicks. Surely not all of her bones were broken. No one could break all of them.

Amri carefully unwrapped the blankets and revealed Keseke's khiton. It was soaked in blood. Her limbs were bent in too many places, some with the broken ends of bones sticking out through wounds.

"Rivai, go and summon the healer," I said as I went to her side. I would have taken her hand in mine, but her fingers were shattered.

Amri said something to Rivai that I could not hear,

and they both went outside for a time. Only the spice merchant returned, with a vial of sweet-smelling liquid.

"This is made from parts of a flower, the juice of which can take away great pain," he told me as he gently held the vial to Keseke's lips. "Only a few drops are needed for most pains. A whole vial will remove all her pain forever." He looked at me but made no move to give her the liquid.

I understood what he was asking. I was no healer, but even I could see that there was no hope. Her body would never recover from such injuries. Still, I wanted to smash the vial out of his hand, and scream at him, and curse the Adonai for permitting this to happen to my friend.

I did none of those things. I did the thing that was right, and merciful. "Give her the full vial."

He tipped the liquid into her mouth.

Keseke swallowed it and then opened one eye. "Red flower juice. My thanks."

Amri murmured a blessing over her.

"I thought I would not see you again," she said, looking up at me. Her voice was a raw, ruined sound. "I planned not to."

I choked back a sob. "Your plans never do seem to work out well."

"I did not ask for you," she said. "I was afraid his men were watching the gate and would see you. That is why I asked for your brother."

"Did Nabal do this to you?"

She nodded and coughed. "I almost got away with

it. Almost. Another inch and I would have slit his throat, but for that slut Edomite screaming."

"You tried to kill Abigail's husband?" Amri asked.

"Someone has to," she told him. Her voice was growing slurred. "I shall speak to Abigail alone now."

Amri left us. I placed my hand on the top of Keseke's head, stroking her dry, brittle hair. "Why did you do this?"

"Someone has to," she repeated. "You must listen to me now, Mistress. My life does not matter anymore. There are others in danger."

My parents, Rivai. "Whom will my husband harm next?"

"The leader of the dal who guard Yehud's camp sent men to speak to the master this morning. The kitchen wench overheard it all and told it to me. These men greeted the master in Melekh David's name and wished peace on him and his household. They told how his shepherds were guarded by the dal, who did not hurt them or steal from them, and that Yehud and the herdsmen would attest to this. They asked that he find favor with them, as they had come on a feast day, and to give them enough food to last them a week, so they could make their journey out of Paran."

I wanted to scream. How could David do such a foolish thing? *By believing your tale of a generous husband*, my heart told me. "Nabal turned them away."

"He was yet drunk from the night before when they came. He laughed at them and insulted them.

He called them liars and thieves, and Melekh David a runaway slave." She paused to cough, and I saw more blood appear on her lips. "One of the Nabal's guards followed them back to the dal's encampment. They are but two hours away from here. They repeated the master's foolish insults to Melekh David, and he ordered them to strap on their swords and ready themselves for battle. He is coming tonight with all four hundred men to kill the master and every member of his household."

I thought of the shearing sheds, so near the house of my husband. Yehud and his sons would still be there working. "No."

Keseke clutched at my khiton with her broken fingers. "You must go there now, and warn everyone to flee, while there is still a chance."

"Hush now." I wiped some blood trickling from the corner of her mouth. "Why did he have you beaten like this?"

"I failed him, and I tried to kill him." She gave me a strange smile, her one eye turning dark from the effects of the juice. "But I did not fail you, did I, Mistress?"

"No, my friend." I bent to her and put my arms around her, careful not to jostle her broken limbs. "I knew you would not."

"Then I can rest. Go, Abigail. Go before he comes and . . ." She released a choked breath, then another, and went limp in my arms.

I closed her eyes with my hand and tenderly eased her down upon the bloodstained blankets. I prayed

over her and anointed her brow with oil. "Adonai, bless her soul and forgive her sins. She did not fail me or You."

Amri promised to watch over Keseke's body for me until a proper kispu could be arranged. Outside I spoke with my brother, who demanded to know who Keseke was and why she had been beaten so.

"She owed a debt to my husband, and he collected it this way," I told him.

"I shall go to the shofet—"

"No, there is no time. I must go out into the valley of the crossroads." I looked and saw Amri's empty wagon, and his mule cropping some grass near the opening to Amri's stockroom. "Bring Amri's mule here and hitch it for me. I shall take that."

Rivai caught my shoulders. "Abigail, you cannot leave now."

I looked up at him. "Rivai, for once, I beg you, do as I say." When he did not release me, I shoved him aside and went to hitch up the mule myself.

"You are doing it wrong." He came and took the harness straps from me. "Father will kill me if anything happens to you."

I did not answer him. I thought only of going to David and confronting him. I would make him see that he could not kill innocent people in his anger. As I pulled my samla tightly around me, I cursed Nabal and David. They cared nothing for the lives of Yehud, his sons, or the dal. They were both arrogant fools.

In that moment, words I had heard before whispered inside my mind: *One king fool, one fool king.*

The prophecy of the m'khashepah—but how could she have known that I would now be caught between such men?

Whose shall you be? Whose truth shall you speak?

Lightning flashed in the sky overhead, although there were no storm clouds or sign of rain. Rivai cringed and then looked up. "What was that?"

I was lost in the words of the m'khashepah, remembering everything she had predicted. *Seek mercy where none is deserved. Cry mercy when none is earned. Stand and you shall fall. Kneel and you shall rise. Search for it, bargain for it, crawl for it. . . .*

I could not be sure of the meaning. What was happening now might have nothing to do with her words. There was one possibility, but it meant that I had to give both men not what they desired but what they deserved.

When you doubt, go back to the wheel. Turn the wheel.

"I need the clay first," I said to myself.

"Abigail, what are you talking about? You do not need clay at a time like this." Rivai looked frightened. "What is wrong? Why are your eyes so wild?"

I took his hand and held it so that I could climb up onto the wagon. "I may not return. Tell Mother and Father and Cetura that I love them dearly. As I do you, Brother."

I could still hear Rivai shouting after me as I drove the wagon through the city gate and took the road leading to Maon.

*   *   *

I did not drive the wagon up to the front of Nabal's house. I was determined, but I would do no
one any good dead. Instead, I drove it around to the
back, where the shearing sheds stood.

I found Yehud and his sons eating a hastily prepared meal in the midst of the bundled fleeces they
had shorn that day. The smell of wet wool and lye
was thick in the air, and the men wore shearing
clothes so covered with bits of wool and dirt that I
hardly recognized them.

Yehud rose when he saw me. "Abigail? Have you
gone mad?" He looked up toward the house and
back at me. "You cannot be here. Your friend, the
serving woman, was beaten and dragged from here.
Your husband has vowed to do the same to you the
moment he sees you."

"Rosh, there are more important things amiss now.
Please, can you tell me what was said between my
husband and David's men?"

"David sent his messengers to greet our master,
and we went to stand with them, as they have become our friends these past months," one of Yehud's
sons said, "but he reviled them. We told the master
that the men were very good to us while we grazed
his flocks in Paran, and that as long as we accompanied them when we were in the fields, not a single
animal went missing."

"I did not ask for them, but they were a wall to
us day and night," Yehud agreed. "This I told Master
Nabal, and he only laughed and said it was free ser-

vice. There is nothing to be done, child. If David means to harm our master, it would be his due. He is such a fool and a scoundrel that one cannot speak to him."

I had no time to deal yet with my husband. "I need you and your sons to help me load this wagon."

"What do you put into it?"

"That which might persuade David not to attack."

As I suspected, there was no one but the kitchen servant inside preparing food, and red blotches from weeping still covered her face. When I came in with the herdsmen, she squeaked with alarm.

"You must not be here," she warned, trying to push me back through the door. "The master wishes you dead."

"Do not cry out my name," I told her. "Where is my husband's steward?"

"He has gone into town to gamble. He stays the night with a woman there." She saw Yehud's sons carry sacks out of the storage room. "What are you doing?"

"We are taking what we need," I said. "Say nothing to the master of this."

"But you cannot take all of that," she wailed. "He will find it missing and have me beaten as Keseke was."

"I shall be back in the morning to give him what he is due," I promised her. "For now, you should go and stay in the shearing sheds. Yehud's sons will protect you there."

There was too much to fit into one wagon, so I

sent three of Yehud's sons to appropriate more mules from Nabal's stables. Yehud helped me to finish packing the wagon and the mules and then regarded me silently.

"He shall not kill me," I promised him. "Not right away."

"You understand how proud David is." Yehud gestured to the wagon. "This may not be enough, Abigail."

"It is not all that I mean to give." I took one of the mules and climbed onto its back, settling myself between the heavy packs suspended from its saddle. "Send the others and the wagon after me. I must go now if I am to stop them in time."

I slapped the reigns and started the mule toward Paran, and David.

CHAPTER

18

I did not reach David's encampment in time to stop the army from marching. I met them halfway to Maon, coming up the road in orderly ranks. I had never seen them all together before, and although they were thin and poorly dressed, each man carried a spear, a sword or knife, and a shield.

I saw them from the top of a hill. They did not see me, or did not care that I was in their path, for they did not stop moving forward. I guided the mule down the sloping road, and then stopped and looked back toward Maon. I could see the other mules and the wagon slowly making their way toward us; they would arrive in a few minutes.

That gave me time to speak to him. I could not speak to him as we had at the spring. He was no longer the shepherd who had sung to me and danced in the rain. He was David, warrior son of Jesse, anointed by Samuel, blessed by the Adonai.

He was my king.

I removed my head cloth and replaced it with the one I had taken from the kitchen girl at my husband's house. I had never worn the head cloth of a servant, but I draped it as a servant would wear and started forward, guiding the mule toward the army.

I heard David speaking to one of his captains as I approached.

"You would think we had raided his flocks, instead of protecting them," the captain was saying.

"Surely in vain I have protected all that this Nabal has in Paran, so that he lost nothing," David said. "And this is how he repays me, with evil for good. May the One and True God do so, and more also, to my enemies, if by morning light I leave one male of all who belong to him." He stopped as he caught sight of me on the mule, and called the army to halt.

I dismounted quickly from the mule and hurried forward to prostrate myself before him. I did not merely kneel; I lay facedown at his feet, the most humbling position I knew. "Let this iniquity be upon me, my lord."

He reached down for me. "Get up."

I did not move. "Please, let your maidservant speak to you, and hear my words." His hands left my arms, and I continued as if we were complete strangers. "Please, my lord, do not give any regard to this scoundrel, Nabal. For as his name means fool, so is he a fool bent on folly."

The mention of my husband's name made him hiss something under his breath.

"You must understand, my lord, that I, your maid-

servant, did not see the young men whom you sent to my husband. As the Adonai lives, so you live. I know He has held you back from coming to bloodshed and from avenging yourself with your own hand. Let your enemies and those who seek to harm you be as Nabal. Fools engaged in folly."

"What do you ask of me?" I heard him ask through clenched teeth.

"To give this present which your maidservant has brought to you." By now he surely saw the packs on my mule, and the others coming over the hill. "Let it be given to the young men who follow you, my lord, as your army. Please forgive the trespass of your maidservant for not attending to you and your needs. For the Adonai shall certainly make for you an enduring house, because you fight the Adonai's battles, and no evil will be found in you throughout your days."

"A house cannot endure with a dead master," David said softly.

He was telling me that King Saul still hunted him. "A man pursues you and seeks your life, but you are wrapped in the arms of the Adonai. The lives of your enemies He shall sling out, as you have sent rocks from the pocket of your sling. It shall come to pass," I said, lifting my face to look upon his. "When the Adonai has done as He has promised for you, and has appointed you ruler over Israel, that this matter will be no grief to you, nor offense of heart to you, either that you have shed blood without cause, or that you have avenged yourself."

I knew what I was asking of him. To remind him that he was better than this, above personal, petty vengeance, was a risk. It was also the only way I could salve his pride.

"I say again, maidservant," he said, "what do you ask of me?"

I could demand nothing. What food I had brought might satisfy the debt my husband owed him, but what David and I had shared could not be satisfied. We would forever be in debt to each other.

I pressed my cheek to his feet and closed my eyes. "I ask only that when the Adonai has dealt well with you, my lord, that you might remember your maidservant."

My memory was the only thing I could give him now.

I did not resist David's hands as he drew me to my feet. I dared not look into his eyes. He might strike me and cast me aside for daring to come to him. He might toss me to the nearest man and have me bound and gagged so that I would give no warning to Nabal.

"Abigail."

I barely heard the whisper, but it brought my eyes to his.

Still holding my hands, he smiled down at me. "Blessed is the Adonai, the One and True, who sent you this day to meet me."

I did not dare ask him what he meant. I only held onto his hands and waited.

"And blessed is your advice and blessed are you,

because you have kept me this day from coming to bloodshed and from avenging myself with my own hand." He turned to face his men. "For indeed, as the Adonai lives, He has kept us back." As the men cheered, he lowered his voice. "You were very bold, but very wise, little dove. Had you not hurried and come to meet me, I would have left no man in that house alive."

"I know, my lord." I let out a long breath. "Yehud and his sons are there shearing. I did not think they would have been recognized in time to be spared."

David went still. "I swear to you, I did not know them to be there, Abigail."

"That is why I came." I stepped back and bowed low. "Your maidservant thanks you, my lord."

His men were surrounding us, exclaiming over what I had brought for them on the mules. Yehud's sons came to greet their friends and called to David.

I looked into his eyes and saw his frustration. "I must go, my lord," I said.

"Then go up in peace to your house," he told me. "I have heeded your voice and respected your person."

I would have gladly thrown myself back at his feet and begged to stay with him as his servant, but there was other work left to be finished. I bowed again and went to my mule, which had been unloaded. Together we started back for Maon.

I thought a great deal before I reached my husband's property. I thought of David, who had shown

himself to be all that was said of him, and more. My praise had not been solely for the benefit of his men or in vain. His actions proved beyond a doubt that he would be a great king, and his house would endure with the blessings of the Adonai.

Did David know me better now? Had I proven myself to be what I truly was? What was that? Who had I become?

A common potter's daughter with the cold and calculating heart of a merchant. A liar and thief who dared to bargain with a king to save the life of a wealthy, evil fool.

That was my truth, and that was what people would remember of me whenever my name was spoken.

I did not like knowing myself like this. I had not been this, before Nabal. He had shaped me into this thing that I had become.

The mule was tired and only moved faster than a walk when it saw the front gate. I stopped the mule there and tied it to a post so that I could walk the remaining distance to the house.

It was silent, with several of the servants sleeping out by the spits. They must have been exhausted from the long night of providing meat for the feast. Half a carcass still hung from one rod, now a banquet for the flies. More waste in the name of Nabal.

The house was silent as I walked in, but the smell of strong wine and roast meat was still thick in the air. I followed the smell to the great room and had to step over several richly clothed men as I went. The feast must have been a success for my husband's

friends to drink so much that they fell asleep on the floor with the dogs.

One of the Edomites stumbled out of Nabal's bedchamber and directly into my path. She looked at me through bleary eyes ringed with smeared blue paint. "The master will see you dead this day." She smirked. "Then he will give me your garments to wear."

I might have drawn my hand back and struck her full across the mouth, but she was really no different from me. Her crime was in selling herself so cheaply. Part of me understood her eagerness to bed Nabal, too. "Do you yet carry my husband's child?"

Her mouth pouted. "Soon he will plant a son in my belly while you rot in the ground."

"I would not try on robes or choose names as yet," I advised as I moved past her and into the great room.

More men were piled on cushions and floor mats, nearly all in drunken slumber. One stalwart young man was doing his best to rouse the other Edomite, but she snored through his ardent caresses.

My husband was the grandest spectacle in the room. To entertain his friends, he had worn his finest robes, intricately embroidered vestments like those the holy priests wore to the ceremonies at the bamot. A bejeweled circlet of pure gold glittered on his hairless head, and his eyes were outlined in kohl in Egyptian fashion. Something swayed, hanging from his two chins, and it took a moment to realize it was

one of the false beards fashioned of turquoise, as worn by the pharaohs.

He was not asleep or drunk. He was waiting and smiling pleasantly.

"Friends, business partners, debtors," my husband announced loudly, startling some of the sleeping men. "Greet my new and very errant wife, Abigail, late of Carmel." He clapped his hands, and waited.

It woke the Edomite, who shrieked and pushed the man atop her to one side, but no one else came into the room.

"Where is my steward?" Nabal rose from his chair and clapped his hands together, this time louder. "Takis! Attend me."

"He is in town, Master," the Edomite said, slapping at the eager hands of her admirer. "The others are out sleeping by the cooking pits."

"Go and wake them," he told her. "I have need of two stout men, a length of rope, and my cudgel."

The Edomite gathered up her robe and held it to cover her naked front as she hurried out.

By now the other men in the room had awaken, and were looking from Nabal's benign smile to me. With muttered excuses and hasty thanks, my husband's friends rose and left, one by one, until we were alone.

"I did not think you would dare return," Nabal said. "The debts from those dog merchants in Carmel made me angry." He looked up as the Edomite peered around the door. "Well? Where are they?"

"They are afraid to come," she whined, "because of what happened the last time you sent for such things."

I thought of Keseke, dying in my arms. Of Malme, and how close she had come to death. Of Rivai, and the crushing weight of a debt he had been tricked into assuming. Of Nabal's family, killed in the middle of the night so that he could have all that was theirs for himself.

No more lives would be sacrificed on the altar of my husband's greed.

I went to the door and shoved the Edomite's face out before I closed it and dropped the bar. No one else would intrude.

"So I must do this myself. Lazy servants, I shall dismiss them all later." He stepped down from the platform surrounding his chair. "How was your time in the hills? Did those goatherds teach you anything about how to please a man?"

I met him in the center of the room. Despite his finery, it was evident that he had grown fatter and whiter of skin since the last time I had laid eyes on him. Before this he had only been mildly repulsive, that much I could admit to myself, and now he resembled the maggots that infested old meat.

As he raised his fist to strike me, I smiled. "Men came to see you yesterday. Men to whom you owed a debt."

"I saw no such men." He lowered his fist and picked a particle of food from between his front teeth, flicking it at my feet. "I remember some runaway slaves who came without invitation. They sput-

tered some nonsense about my flocks, but they were obviously beggars. I threw them out of the house."

I would not scream at him. I would not. "Those men you insulted and turned away belong to David, son of Jesse, the anointed of Israel. Do you know who he is?"

"Some outlaw shepherd who desires the throne. The king wants his head." Nabal shrugged. "What of him?"

"The men came back to David and repeated your insults. He called his army of four hundred to arms and ordered them to gird themselves with their swords. To march upon you and your house. To come here and slay you, Nabal, and every man of your household."

My husband jerked back. "By Adonai, you brainless woman, go summon the shamar. They might be at the gates now—I shall not be slain by outlaws under my own roof."

"There is no need to summon anyone, for David has called back his men and returned to his camp."

"What?" His eyes narrowed. "Why?"

"I went to them in the night. I spoke to the man who will be our king. I threw myself at his feet and called myself his servant. I pleaded with him to spare your household and made an offering to sway him."

"The runaway slave king?" He laughed. "What could a little nothing like you offer him? Not the stingy joys to be found in your arms."

"I offered what you owed him, my husband. The

food to feed four hundred starving men." I watched his cheeks go ruddy. "Do you wish a proper accounting? I took two hundred loaves of bread, two skins of wine, five sacks of roasted grain, one hundred clusters of raisins, and two hundred cakes of figs. Five carcasses of mutton, your five fattest, already dressed for your feast; those I took, as well. Yehud and his sons merely killed five more to bring to your roasting spits."

His redness deepened to purple and he shook as his voice became a whisper. "You dared steal food from my house? Out from under my very nose? That food that was meant for my feast."

"You did not go hungry last night. There was enough to spare ten times what I took to Melekh David and his army." I did not flinch as he seized the front of my khiton in his fist. "I was wrong, though. It was not the food, nor my obeisance to Melekh David that swayed him. It was my telling him that the future king of all Israel and Judah should not sully his hands with the blood of a fool."

"I shall kill you for this."

"No, Husband, you will not." I pressed my hand against his chest. "For the Adonai came to me last night. He was pleased that I had saved His beloved son David from tainting his purity with your foulness." I sank my fingernails into his robe. "He granted me the power of a curse on your heart, to turn it into stone. Have you felt how heavy it beats this morning? It has already begun."

Nabal's hand went slack and then knocked mine

away so that he could prod his own chest. "No, it is fine. I am fine."

"The Adonai despises thieves and liars, but He cannot abide murderers. You have known this since you were a boy. That is why you are afraid to die, is it not? Why you have no feelings for others? Because you have always known that someday you would be struck down for your crimes."

"I have killed no one!" he screamed in my face.

"Yet your parents' blood cries out for vengeance. So, too, your brother's. Even poor Keseke's. All the people you have cheated and made to go hungry in your service. All those souls hanging from you like blood-filled ticks." I watched the small red veins in his nose and eyes swell. "Do as you will to me, but it will change nothing. Your heart is turning to stone, my husband, and ten days hence you will die. That is my curse and the will of the Adonai."

"You cannot curse me. You are no one, nothing!" Nabal's breathing became panting. "I shall summon my physician." He groped until he found a table and leaned heavily against it. "He will cure me."

I leaned back against the door. "How will he get into the room?"

"Move away from there." He tried to rise and then made a strangled sound. Sweat poured down his purple face. "Lift that bar. Send for help for me. For the love of the Adonai, you are my wife!"

"Yes, I am." I smiled tenderly at him. "And I shall not leave you, husband. Not until I hear your last breath and know my curse is fulfilled."

Nabal fell against the table, making the dishes on it clatter as his body went into a jerking fit. He fell over atop the remains of his last feast and did not move again.

EPILOGUE

I waited by my husband's bedside for ten days. I waited for him to speak, to move, to do anything to show that he was still the master and I, the wife who had cursed him, would suffer for what I had done.

Nabal did not speak, did not move, did not twitch.

His eyes stared up at the ceiling beams. His mouth hung slack on one side, and saliva dribbled down his neck. When he was fed anything, even a tiny sip of clear broth, he would choke on it.

I was the one to feed him, for most of his servants had run off, frightened by what I had done. The steward, who was not as superstitious, informed me that he was leaving, and took a good deal of Nabal's gold with him when he did. I did not care. It was not my gold, and after all the years he had served my husband, he likely had earned it.

Rivai came on the eighth day to plead with me.

"Come home, Abigail. There is nothing you can do for him."

I would not speak. The last words that had come from my lips had done this thing to Nabal. I would not speak again until it was finished.

"Why do you keep silent? Why do you stay?"

I could not tell him that it was the pact I had made with the Adonai. If Nabal lived, I would be wife to him and care for him, no matter in what state his body was left. I would accept whatever punishment he gave, be it my own death.

All I had to do was wait and see how it would be.

My brother argued and pleaded and shouted, but I was not moved. At last he left, exasperated beyond words with me.

I kept my silence, and my vigil.

At dawn on the tenth day, Nabal's breathing changed. By the time the sun rose, his chest barely moved at all. I watched without blinking as the pulse in his thick neck slowed and faltered. The last breath he took escaped like a sigh, and then he breathed no more.

So I was wife no more, but widow.

I cannot say all that happened to me after Nabal died. I remember walking from his chamber and through the empty house. I took nothing, not even the things that were mine. I was not conscious of being, only of moving, and walking.

There was my walking, a great deal more, out of Maon and into the wide fields, now shorn of their

wheat. I passed gleaners picking through the stubble, and heard someone call a greeting to me. I did not answer. I walked beyond those eyes, and that voice.

I walked all of that day and night, and into the next morning. I walked until I fell down into the soft, green grass, and closed my eyes, and slept. When I woke, I stood and began walking again.

Hunger gnawed at me, but it was a distant thing. Sometimes I walked through nettles, or brushed past bushes laden with thorns. The stings and hurts they inflicted on me faded to nothing. When cramps seized my legs, I would lie down and wait for them to pass. When I could walk no more, I lay down and slept.

Bethel told me that I walked into camp at noon. My khiton hung in shreds, and scratches and filth covered my body. I walked directly to her, and fell at her feet, and could not rise again.

Yehud's women took me into their tent and washed me like an infant. They wept over me and prayed the kispu for me. One of the men was sent to Carmel to tell my family that I was dying.

But I did not die. I slept.

Bethel scolded the mourning women and tried to rouse me. When she could not, Leha later told me, she ordered that I be attended night and day.

The old woman herself sat beside me and held my hand and talked to me as if I still had my senses. She fed me thin porridge for many days, as nothing else would stay down. When she grew tired, Leha or one of the other women came and took her place.

One morning I woke and knew myself and my sanity again. I opened my eyes to see Bethel sitting beside me, her hand gently drawing a comb through my hair. "You make a habit of this, girl," she was muttering, "and I shall beat you."

"Wife of Yehud," I whispered.

"Widow of Nabal." She bent over to look into my eyes. "So you have come back to us again."

"I bring you only grief this time."

"No, beloved Abigail." She set aside the comb and looked down at me with love in her eyes. "You bring that which is always with you. Joy."

Although the women of the camp had nursed me well, I was horribly weak, and it took another day and night before I could rise from my sleeping mat, even for a brief time. Bethel, worried I might take it into my head to go walking into the desert, insisted that Leha act as my shadow.

I did not mind. If there was a balm for my spirit, it was Leha's soft voice and gentle smile.

Leha first walked with me around the camp, which was all my strength would allow. Where we went, there were smiles and nods. Everyone seemed happy to see me, but I did not know why.

"My uncle took our finest ram to the bamot in Maon," Leha told me. "He called upon the Adonai to bless you and your house for the rest of your days. What you did, Abigail . . ." She shook her head. "I do not have the words."

I thought of Nabal's empty, staring eyes. "I have

no more house nor husband. There will be no children, and I shall die gerusa."

"You do not know, then. I was not certain if you heard us speaking of it; you were so ill." Leha stopped and faced me. "We sent word to Carmel ere you came here and your brother drove out to see you. He could not stay, for he told us that after you disappeared, the shofet of Maon entrusted your husband's estate upon your family. They are keeping it for you until you return, but it is yours, Abigail."

"I want nothing of my husband's."

Leha made a helpless gesture. "By law it is yours."

"By law I should be stoned to death for killing him," I said, my voice harsh.

We had come to the edge of the forest and the path that led to the spring. I stared at it and recalled the many, happy times I had walked here.

Leha turned and listened carefully, and then said, "I think I hear my aunt calling for me." She handed me the jug she carried. "Will you draw the water, Abigail?"

I nodded and took the jug before I started down the path to the spring.

Each step drove some of the numbness from my heart, replacing it with a pain so acute I felt it like a knife. For here was the place where I had fallen in love with my fool king, and here I had offered myself to him out of love. It was not tainted with my sin, this place. It was free of everything but the sweetest of memories.

I went through the gap, shedding my clothing as I did. Naked as a newborn, I stood by the edge of the waters.

I looked at the sky. "Adonai, hear me. In all things I have done Your will. I have been the generous one. I have given all that I have for love and honor. There is no more left of me to give now, and I would that you forgive me my sins and let me be as a child in Your eyes."

I filled the jug and lifted it over my head, and poured it over myself. The water was cold against my heated skin, but as it rushed down my body, I felt the crushing weight of Nabal's death ease. Perhaps there was forgiveness for one such as I.

I squeezed the wetness from my hair, refilled the jug, and turned to retrieve my clothes.

David stood at the entrance to the spring, straight and tall, his black hair gleaming with blue in the sun.

I studied him. "You are staring."

"I am." He did not move from his place. "I have scoured nearly all of Judah, looking for you." He held out my shift and khiton.

"I went walking. I was not myself for a time. The Adonai guided my feet to bring me here." I went to him and took my clothes, but I did not hurry to dress. "Nabal is dead."

"We had word of it. That is why I searched for you." He took my shift back and pulled it over my head. "You are very thin, Abigail of Paran."

The name startled me, but suddenly it felt right. I

was no longer tied to Carmel or Maon or any town. "You look tired, Melekh David."

"Searching for a little dove in the great, wide wilderness is exhausting. And frustrating." He stared down at me. "I am yet a hunted man. The king has not forgiven me for whatever he imagines my crimes. I have taken the men to Ziklag, where Samuel's kin will give us sanctuary. We still must live as nomads and take work where we can find it."

It was not fair. "I am sorry for that."

He helped me into my khiton. "There will be work—and pay for it—for us in Ziklag. I have given the men permission to send for their wives and children." He touched my cheek. "You are thinner, but your eyes have not changed. They are yet as cool and peaceful as the waters of Bethlehem. My sleeping mat is empty, Abigail. I dream alone."

"What are you saying?" I whispered.

"I shall return to my men now. There are two of them I must send back to this place, to speak to Yehud about a marriage."

Doubtless one of his men, wishing to wed one of Yehud's daughters. I did not want to think about marriage. The wrench of losing him yet again to his duty was making me bleed inside. "I wish you good journey."

"I would know if Yehud will give his blessing to the match." He brushed a piece of wet hair back from my brow. "Perhaps you can advise me."

"Who is this man?"

"Some call him an outlaw, but he is in truth only a shepherd. He has an unruly temper and needs to be reminded of his purpose when it becomes snarled. He is poor, too." He linked his hands with mine. "Someday that will change, but for now, all he can give her is his heart."

"And who is this woman?" I asked quietly.

"A widow recent, but the kindest, gentlest heart in Judah. She is not afraid of work or sacrifice. She was raised in town, but learned to live in the wilderness. She protects life, even if it means lying facedown in the road before an arrogant fool and calling herself a maidservant."

I choked out a laugh. "She is hardly more than that."

"I would rather see her a wife to the man who needs her rather more than breathing. The man to whom she was sent by the Adonai, over and over again." He tilted his head. "What is your advice, then? Should my men come to speak to the rosh about this union? Or is it a hopeless matter, better forgotten?"

I drew my hands from his to pick up the jug of water, which I propped against my hip. With my free hand I covered my head, and turned to go. I knew I would sleep well this night, and there would be no more dreams of longing. My dream lived.

My dream also patiently awaited an answer, so I looked back and gave it to him. "Send your men, Melekh David."

AFTERWORD

Abigail, one of the most notable women in the Bible, lived in Judah more than three thousand years ago. All we know about her is the description of a confrontation between her and David, the future king of Israel, in the twenty-fifth chapter of Samuel. From the Scriptures, we have the story of how Abigail saved the lives of many innocent people by persuading a proud and very angry David not to take personal vengeance on her foolish husband, Nabal, and his household.

That Abigail was courageous goes without question. How many women would, by themselves, try to stop an army of four hundred men? Yet what has always fascinated me about Abigail is what we do not know about her. We know she came from Carmel, but we have no information about her family, or under what circumstances she was raised. We do not know why such a wise woman who possessed such exemplary communication skills was married to

a man who was as foolish as he was greedy. We also do not really know why David listened to her advice. Abigail's appeal to him was beautifully spoken, but the gist of what she says is mostly praise for David (1 Samuel 25: 23–31).

Was the future king of Israel actually manipulated by flattery from a quick-thinking, fast-talking woman? Or did Abigail pull off the very first peace talks ever initiated and negotiated by a woman? I leave that for my readers to decide.

I took many, many liberties with Abigail's story, including adapting passages from the Holy Bible and inventing a private life for David, a charismatic and important figure who is surpassed only by Moses and Abraham for the number of times he is mentioned in the Bible. I would like to remind my readers that although this novel was built on firm foundations of fact, it was designed from the ground up by pure imagination. Thus, nothing of Abigail's story should be carved in stone, or someone will probably pitch it through one of my windows.

Ann Burton
September 1, 2004

GLOSSARY OF TERMS

Author's note: The actual Hebrew form of the following words has very complicated accenting and punctuation. In a few cases, some of the letters used to spell these words do not exist in the English alphabet. To make the text of this novel reader-friendly, I have removed all of the accenting, punctuation marks, and non-English letters from these words.

Adonai: Lord, a term used in place of Yahweh or God

Adonai yireh: Lord, protect us

bahur: young unmarried man

bamot: high place or temple used for worship

bet ab: the father's house

betulah: unmarried virgin woman

dal: poor; people who have lost prosperity and family

erwat dabar: feces or other unclean matter found in a camp

ezor: undergarment worn by men

ger: outsider (plural: gerum)

gerusa: divorced women cast off by their husbands

go'el: family member designated to pay debts when
other members of the family cannot

hagor: belt, worn to keep the ezor in place

horoi: stones marking the boundary of nahalah

Issah nokriyah: foreign (non-Hebrew) woman

khiton: outer garment, like a robe

kor: unit of measure, roughly equal to a donkey-load

kushtha: medicinal herb; aka Costus

lehem: bread

maneh: weight measure used as money; 1 maneh =
50 sheqels

Melekh: the anointed King, chosen by the Adonai

m'khashepah: witch or occultist

mohar: bride price, paid to a bride's family

nahalah: plot or parcel of land belonging to a family

noqed: keepers and raisers of sheep; herdsmen

pesel: graven image or idol

qahal: assembly

quern: saddle-shaped stone used for grinding

rea: neighbor

sadhin: kiltlike garment worn on the hips

Shabbat: the Sabbath

shamar: guardsmen

sheqel: weight measure used as money; 50 sheqels =
1 maneh

shofar: ram's horn, blown like a trumpet

shofet: leader (plural: shofetim)

samla: outer robe worn by women

simla: outer robe worn by men

tola'at shani: red dye made from the scarlet worm

yeled: newborn, infant

zaqen: elder

zebed: dowry, given to a bride's husband

DISCUSSION GUIDE

1. The family was the foundation of rural society in Ancient Israel. Compare Abigail's family to your own: What about them is different, or similar? What advantages or disadvantages does family give to a person in today's world?

2. Mosaic law curtailed the activities of women like Abigail and forced them to live sheltered lives. What would it be like to live under such restrictions? What are some of the restrictions modern women encounter in your country? Are such restrictions methods to safeguard or control women?

3. In Abigail's time, a family member called a go'el was required by law to pay any debts that another member of the family could not. What is the equivalent of a go'el in our time? While today it is no longer a legal requirement to act as go'el,

should family members still help each other with their debts? Why?

4. Shepherds appear in many stories from the Bible, and many characters from the Bible once lived as shepherds. Why are shepherds such an important and enduring symbol? Who are the shepherds of our time, and what have they done to make our lives better?

5. The story of David and Goliath illustrates how courage and ingenuity can often defeat strength and bravado. Can you think of other battles that have taken place between similarly mismatched opponents? Who won those battles, and why?

6. Half of the women who gave birth in Ancient Israel died of complications following childbirth. Today, conditions for expectant mothers in some countries are little better than they were three thousand years ago. What can be done to help these countries improve maternal and infant mortality rates? How can better education help improve the health of pregnant women?

7. The worshipping and making of graven images were forbidden among Abigail's people so that they would not be tempted to pay homage to false gods. What practices are taboo in your culture or religion? Why are these important? Which would you change, and why?

8. Abigail compares many things in her life to the making of pottery. Apply aspects of your work or hobbies to life in general. What wisdom can you draw from them? How might they help other people live better and make wiser decisions?

9. David was King Saul's acknowledged successor, and yet the king was jealous and suspicious of him, and tried to kill him. David, however, refused to strike back. What do you think was the reason behind Saul's behavior? Was David right in not trying to retaliate?

10. Abigail's story is about the price of family love, generosity, and pride. Which character from the story do you most sympathize with? Which character was most at fault? How would you have handled Abigail's dilemmas?

RECOMMENDED READING

Families in Ancient Israel, by Leo G. Perdue, Joseph Blenkinsopp, John J. Collins, and Carol Meyers, published by Westminster John Knox Press, ISBN# 0-664-25567-1

Life in Biblical Israel, by Philip J. King and Lawrence E. Stager, published by Westminster John Knox Press, ISBN# 0-664-22148-3

The Everything Jewish History & Heritage Book, by Richard D. Bank and Julie Gutin, published by Adams Media Corporation, ISBN# 1-58062-966-0

What Did the Biblical Writers Know & When Did They Know It: What Archaeology Can Tell Us About the Reality of Ancient Israel, by William G. Dever, published by Wm. E. Eerdmans Publishing Company, ISBN# 0-8028-2126-X

Excerpt from *Women of the Bible: Rahab's Story*

By Ann Burton

Coming from Signet in September 2005

I wandered the streets of Jericho, knowing not where I walked or caring much of my direction. What did it matter where I ended? I had been publicly shamed, shorn. From this day forth, I was forever outcast among my kin. I would never again be known as Rahab, eldest daughter of Robur the rug seller, sister of Tezi, or even Rahab the weaver. My stepmother's jealousy and lies had reduced me to Rahab the witch, Rahab the pariah. I reached up and touched the uneven stubble covering my scalp; my hair had been my only real beauty, and she had even taken that from me.

Rahab the outcast. Rahab the bald.

I turned corners and walked through archways, uncaring where they led me, deaf to the jeers and

laughter of those who spied my shorn head and enjoyed my humiliation. There was a numb logic to my movement. I had nowhere to go. Where I stopped, I would drop. Where I dropped, I would likely die. If I wanted to end it quickly, all I had to do was find a guardsman and confess to being a Semite. He would probably take some initiative and behead me on the spot.

No, I could not even give myself that ghastly but swift end. Word of my confession might travel, or people might recognize my face from upon whichever pike they left my head. Word that might lead the city guard back to my home. Although I cared little for a father who had so readily abandoned me, and nothing for Helsbah, I could not let them take Tezi.

I might die out here, alone and reviled, but my silence would buy my little sister life.

Some unconscious part of me guided my feet toward the southeast corner of the city, to Meshnedef. It was an appropriate destination, this place of lost hope, the one quarter to which my mother had always forbidden me go. In Meshnedef, she had told me, the poorest of the city dwelled in perpetual filth and squalor, ever preyed upon by thieves and madmen. Decent folk never walked its dark and narrow streets, which Mother claimed ran thick with offal and rats, or patronized its shops, which Mother assured me only sold diseased meat and stolen goods.

I became aware of my surroundings only shortly

after I had crossed into Meshnedef. It was as if I had stepped over an invisible line that divided the virtuous from the reprehensible, the decent from the licentious. Not that there were written warnings posted, or guardsmen to keep the rabble from intruding on the respectable. Yet the signs were all around me, from the deplorable condition of the unpaved, pitted road to the rotten thatch of the roofs sagging overhead.

The first things I noticed were the little piles of scat, fresh and old, whole and smeared, that littered the street. Some obviously had been left behind by the four-legged, but others, dropped in nooks and corners, surely had been deposited by those who walked on two.

Raised in a house with an old-fashioned but functional privy, I found the sight repugnant and rather unbelievable. Even in the poorest neighborhoods of my quarter, there were public rest houses for servants and latrine pits for slaves. Were there none here? If not, still, how could one simply relieve oneself so openly, out here in the street?

A pair of skinny stray dogs trotted past me, not bothering to sniff at my hem, intent on a rat slinking out from a pile of rubbish. They cooperated as they went at it, one cornering and driving the rat out to the other.

Caught as I was between Helsbah and Meshnedef, I could sympathize with the rat.

The chase was silent but brief, and only when its wriggling body lay clenched between the jaws of one

dog did the other explode with sharp, indignant barking. The rat catcher swallowed his prize with two jerks of his head and ran off, pursued by his unhappy, unsatisfied companion.

If I were to die in the gutter with those two, I thought, recalling Helsbah's curse, I would likely have something of a wait.

I tried to dispel my gloom by focusing again on my surroundings. Here, nothing appeared to be maintained for even basic sanitary reasons; yet, it was not as bad as Mother had led me to believe. Filth did indeed crowd the gutters, but time and rainwater had reduced it to an anonymous sludge. The houses were small, cramped, and poorly thatched, but as I moved into the market, I saw no diseased meats or goods of any kind. The absence of front stalls offering goods on display—perhaps to remove temptation from passing thieves—made the shops seem somewhat tidier than those at our market. Cool shade came from the shops' proximity to the city's great wall, next to which they were nestled like eggs against a warm feathered breast. The wall itself was wide enough to sport a row of shops high upon its battlements, and formed a barrier against the dry desert wind, which often came in off the sands as scorchingly hot as the sun.

The most striking difference was in the dress of the people of Meshnedef. Few walked the street, and those who did ignored me. I saw no signs of wealth, no fine jewels or collars or medallions of any kind.

Indeed most of the men and women who crossed my path wore no ornaments whatsoever, and dressed in very plain, aged robes, the kind my stepmother would have thought only appropriate for scullery servants or slaves.

As I wondered exactly what the inhabitants of Meshnedef did buy, I turned a corner and heard the sound of trickling, splashing water. Sweat broke out prickling over my near-naked scalp, while my throat felt as if I had swallowed a pan filled with hearth sweepings. I had not stopped or rested since leaving my father's house, and my bare feet ached. Perhaps I could beg a drink from the source of the water.

As I followed the sound, I came to the end of the row of shops. There, standing in the deep shadow of the city's Great Wall was a modest structure, two stories in height. Rather than sharing a wall or two with neighboring buildings, as all of the other shops had, it alone occupied the center of a small, barren patch of land.

I saw no fountain, but someone had planted two palms on the sunny side of the house. The sight of them was almost as cooling as a dipper from a well, and I smiled a little a I watched their wide fronds trail green fingers over trumpet-shaped arcs of plump brown dates. Small streams of water trickled over them from an odd sort of irrigation spout hanging over the palms from the roof of the house.

I studied the trees. If I could somehow climb the

nubbly trunks, I might gather a few dates to go along with my drink. "But do I wish to be a beggar, or a thief?"

A pretty laugh rang out behind me. "Gods, child, such dismal choices. Is there nothing else you can do?"

Excerpt from *Women of the Bible: Deborah's Story*

By Ann Burton

Coming from Signet in March 2006

It was through a lush and green garden that I walked, pausing here and there to admire a bloom. Such fragile things, flowers were, and yet they burst forth here as a thousand shofar, trumpeting their colors and beguiling the nose with their sweet scents. Morning dew kissed my toes, and birds chirped merrily to me from their perches on the labyrinth of cedar branches overhead.

I loved this place and came here whenever I could.

Someone had built a fountain in the center of the garden, and that was where I walked now. It was a marvelous thing, carved of polished ivory stone. The water splashing in the basin bubbled up from a hidden spring, so it never ran dry. I scooped some with my hand and brought it to my lips to drink.

"Deborah."

I turned toward the sound. "I am here."

"I have been waiting for you." My love's voice was a warm and wonderful thing that promised laughter and happiness.

I could not see him, but he liked to tease me by hiding. "Where are you?" I left the fountain and began to search for him, smiling as I went. Any moment now, he might jump out and catch me in his arms and whirl me about. "Come out, beloved."

"Deborah." His voice changed. "Deborah, I cannot see you."

The bright sunlight had faded a little, and I looked up to see the sky turning dark with storm clouds. It would rain soon.

"I am here." I pushed aside a tangle of vines. "Come to me, and we will go back into the house." If I could find the way to the house. It had grown so dark I could not see the path leading out of the garden anymore.

"I cannot find you." He sounded anxious. "Deborah, hurry."

Lightning slashed across the black clouds, and wind rushed through the garden to tear at my clothes. I threw up my hands as leaves pelted my face. "I must leave you now. Take shelter."

"Deborah, do not go!"

I turned this way and that, trying to avoid being lashed by the waving branches of the trees. Flowers flew away in the wind, torn from their stems. The light was gone, the sun swallowed by the storm, and I reached out my hand to feel my way.

A hole appeared a few feet away from me, jagged-edged and black as pitch.

A sharp pain struck my shoulder, and I cried out as I fell. I did not want to leave the garden, for it was the only place I felt safe, but I would die if I stayed. "Farewell," I sobbed, crawling toward the ugly scar in the ground. "Farewell, my love."

"Deborah, come back! I will get you to safety! I will get—"

Get.

Get up.

"Do your ears not work?" Something slammed into my shoulder again. "Get up, you lazy slut."

The hard kick knocked me over, so that I lay face-down in the straw. I bit back another cry and quickly curled over, pushing myself up onto my knees.

Ybyon stood over me, his broad face a mask of ugly shadows, his eyes narrow with contempt. "On your feet, girl."

The corner of the barn where I slept was silent, and only the light from the hanging lamp the master carried illuminated the darkness. The others who slumbered next to me in the straw were already gone; I had slept too long again.

"Forgive me, Master," I begged as I stood and tugged my tunic down over my thighs. It hung loosely, for it had once belonged to one of the kitchen wenches. I was given it when it became too stained and threadbare for her to wear. That it was too large did not matter to me. It covered my body, and gave me a little warmth at night when I slept.

Ybyon paused, as if deciding whether to kick me again. "Get to work." He turned and stalked out to the pens.

Because it was so near dawn, I did not dare leave the barn and go to the kitchens for my bread. Instead, I retrieved my pan from where it hung on the wall and carried it to the first stall. The old, bad-tempered spotted goat kept there was eating a pile of scraps from the kitchen refuse heap, and bleated her annoyance as I crouched beside her.

I said nothing when she butted my aching shoulder with her head. I milked her quickly and whisked the pan from beneath her before she could kick it over with her hooves. Her milk warmed the pan and floated, thick and foamy around the edges. I looked from side to side and then bent my head to drink a mouthful before I carried the pan out of the stall.

"Deborah." Meji came and took the pan from me, and looked about before he said in a whisper, "Sorry. I tried to wake you, but you would not move, and then Hlagor shouted for me."

"It matters not." That I had slept too long on a morning that I knew Ybyon would come to inspect the barns and stables was my fault. I had sat up alone last night, watching stars shoot across the sky, when I should have been sleeping. I heard the master's voice drawing close and touched Meji's thin arm before I hurried out to the pens.

Ybyon owned five hundred sheep and two hundred goats, as well as some cows, mules, oxen, and onagers. One of his businesses was the buying and

selling of beasts, so the number occupying the pens and stalls constantly changed. My morning task was to check the sheep pens and see that no lambs had been dropped or injured during the night. In winter I hated going into the pens, for I always found too many of the early births dead of cold or being trampled. Now it was almost spring, I would have to be more vigilant, for the fat ewes would begin dropping their lambs by the dozen each night.

The sheep pen smelled much worse than the barn, and the ground beneath my bare feet was slick with manure. Many of the sheep needed their hooves cut back and cleaned out, for they had grown over, but that would not be done until they were sold. Their wool was thick and greasy to the touch, and their narrow, dark heads turned to look at me as I waded through them.

I saw one of the ewes by the fence, standing as far from the herd as she could manage in the confines of the pen. A stringy, wet mass, the afterbirth from her dropping the lamb that lay curled on the ground under her, hung from beneath her chubby tail.

The lamb was at suck, and the ewe lowered her head as I approached, but I did not disturb them. If I tried to take the lamb now, the ewe would charge me. Instead, I watched the little one have his first meal. I had never known my own mother, so such things drew me.

"Girl!" Ybyon strode toward me, driving the sheep out of his way. "Why do you idle there?"

I bowed my head. "It is a new lamb, Master."

"Yes, yes, I can se that." He clouted the side of my head with his fist. "Why do you not carry it to the lamb pen?"

I cringed and pressed my fingers to my throbbing ear. "It is nursing, Master."

Ybyon reached down, tore the lamb from its mother, and shoved it into my arms. "Now it is not. Take it."

The ewe reacted strongly to this intrusion by charging Ybyon. The master caught her by the neck and spun around, flinging her into the fence. She lay there, stunned and unmoving.

"If she does not rise to go to graze, have one of the shepherds cut her throat," Ybyon told me before he strode out of the pen.

"Yes, Master." I cuddled the bleating lamb close to my chest. I did not dare take him back to his mother to try to rouse her. I never disobeyed Ybyon or questioned what he wished done with his property. No matter how cruel or unfair his orders were, I always carried them out.

I did this because I, too, was Ybyon's property—his slave, from the moment of my birth, just as my mother had been. If I did not do exactly what my master said, he would not send for one of the shepherds to cut my throat.

He would do it himself. As he had when he killed my mother.